COCKY BIKER

COCKER BROTHERS BOOK 2

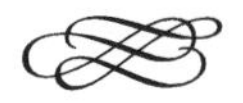

FALEENA HOPKINS

HOP HOP PRODUCTIONS INC.

Cocker Brothers, The Cocky Series.

Hop Hop Productions Inc.

Cover design by Faleena Hopkins

Photos licensed from Shutterstock.com

 Created with Vellum

To the black sheep of the world.
You have a gift for making life more exciting.

I need this wild life, this *freedom*.

— ZANE GREY

For to be free is not merely to cast off one's chains, but to live in a way *that respects and enhances the freedom of others*.

— NELSON MANDELA

LUNA

"When was this coffee made?" I point at the stale and bitter cup of crap.

"Hour ago," is the diner waitress's dry reply.

"Bullshit." I push it toward her.

The back door opens. Strolling into Twain's Diner are five, beefy, dirty-looking bikers wearing matching leather jackets and bad attitudes.

She and I both observe their entrance.

"Shit," she grumbles. "As if my day didn't already suck."

As she walks off with my cup, I call at her back, "Start a new pot, Alice."

Over her shoulder, she snarls, "My name's not Alice."

Like I care.

Striking grey eyes bore into my awareness from the biker with blonde hair. He's locked on me, hot as hell, as his motorcycle club takes up the entire counter on one side, each with a seat between them. I read the patch on their backs: *The Ciphers.*

Spinning stools groan under their muscular weight, and their conversation hasn't stopped. Someone says something about being so hungry he could eat the register, and each takes turns upping the last in weird things to digest. It ends in, "Your balls," and dissolves into guttural laughter.

Fucking dumbasses.

I glance over to Grey Eyes because I feel the stare. It rumbles through my cells and we hold a look so I can drink him in.

Partly I'm pissed he's eyeing me so boldly like he has the right.

Partly because he's fucking hot as hell. Can't help but look. It's been a long time since my body was under a man. Too long.

They're all big. One's pretty ugly—dark hair,

gnarly face. Doesn't look too scary though. Then again, I've looked true evil in the eye.

He notices that Grey Eyes isn't partaking in the convo and glances over his immense shoulder to size me up.

Apparently I win his approval.

Like I give a shit what these guys think of me.

Bikers.

What the fuck.

Sighing impatience, I turn my attention to the window to watch expensive cars drive up and down Coldwater Canyon.

I'm in Los Angeles on business. Not pleasure.

It doesn't matter that Grey Eyes is boring a hole into the side of my head right now.

It sure as fuck doesn't matter that he's that masculine kind of sexy I'd love to melt into if I was another girl.

I don't have time for distractions like him.

Not when I'm this close.

Annoyed as hell, I call over with a dark challenge, "What are you looking at?"

An amused smirk tugs up those smooth lips of his and he keeps right on staring at me.

And says nothing.

Cocky bastard.

Alice hands them menus, but he doesn't turn

around. His buddies greet the waitress with a grunt each.

Luna, stop looking. If you don't put wood on a fire it eventually goes out.

Rummaging through the backpack that carries my whole life, I feel the cool, comforting metal of my 9mm. It's not legal to carry a concealed weapon in California. The evil this is meant for has bigger guns than these. But those machine-gun toting bodyguards will be too late. I have the element of surprise and years of experience sneaking around, on my side.

I get away with bringing this gun with me everywhere.

No one expects a woman to have a weapon.

And if they knew, they'd believe I wouldn't dare use it. How fucking wrong they'd be.

Pulling out the silver pocket watch I stole at fifteen, I read the time and finger the gentle engraving on the back before slipping it into my bag. I had it engraved myself with a one-word promise: *Soon*.

"Five sausages. Double stack of pancakes. That come with potatoes?" Grey Eyes asks Alice. She nods, pen and small ticket book in hand. "What kind?"

"Home fries."

"Extra of those. Four pieces of toast. Two cups of coffee."

Alice raises her penciled-in eyebrows. "Two cups? You don't just want a refill?"

He shakes his head one time. A pudgy, scary-looking fucker to his right is talking under his breath to the guy on the end who can't be older than twenty-two, but who definitely belongs with these dark-souled bastards. He's the tallest of the group, hunching down so he can hear the quiet information being given him.

Outside of the cooks, the only other person in this shithole is an old man with the Los Angeles Times spread out in front of him. What's he got to read about? The perpetually sunny weather? Which star divorced who? The drought? How often can you publish: We Need More Water?

I watch 'Alice' go to the kitchen window to talk to men who look like they could be my family. And there they are slaving away for minimum wage. I will never do that.

One slides a plate at her, and she begrudgingly walks it over to me.

"Thanks," I tell her as she sets down my scrambled eggs and well-done bacon. My show of gratitude (albeit subdued) takes her aback.

She slowly nods, and an understanding rises between us. Unspoken, but we both feel it...I can tell.

"I'll get your coffee." She walks away.

I reach over for the saltshaker. Can't wait to cover my home fries with this. I'm starving.

Haven't eaten since lunch two days ago.

I was so close to finding *him* that I've forgotten to feed myself. When you're obsessed, pausing for anything gets in the way. Even food...until you get so weak you can't function. Which is where I found myself this morning.

The sound of heavy black boots clomping toward me is like a time bomb. Out of my periphery I see thick, muscular thighs walk up.

I sigh and shake the salt over everything on my plate. Even the bacon.

"I don't want company," I mutter.

A steaming cup of fresh caffeine lands in front of my left hand. Grey Eyes slides into the booth with the grace of a lion. You'd think a beast that large wouldn't be able to slink the way it does, but he sure fucking can.

We regard each other in silence. He takes a slow, sexy sip from his own full cup, not giving a shit that it's mouth-burning hot. His lips wrapping around that rim is sexier than it should be. I can't help but watch. He notices my reluctant interest, and licks those lips...deliberately.

"Great," I mutter. "Another cocky fuck who thinks he's God's gift to women."

He pauses and disarms me with a smile so

genuinely entertained that I find myself adjusting my weight in the booth.

Why does this guy make me nervous?

He's as relaxed as if we were lying on a beach with piña coladas in our hands. I glance to his and soak in how thick his fingers are. They say you can judge the size of a man's cock by the size of his hands. I've found that's not true, but you *can* tell the shape of it by his fingers. Grey Eyes has trunks for digits.

"I said I didn't want company," I repeat, glancing over at the low snickers of his friends. They're enjoying this a little too much.

Fuck it.

I grab my backpack and go to leave.

This is a big city.

I'm hungry and salivating now that food is this close to getting in my mouth, but I can find someplace else.

"Hey hey hey." Grey Eyes reaches over. Not all rapey-like. More just surprised and hoping for my patience.

I flinch, so that makes him stop just shy of grabbing my arm.

I don't like to be touched unless I've asked for it.

This is *my* body.

I say who comes near it.

"What?" I demand. "You come over and sit down

like we know each other or something. We don't. And I just want to eat my breakfast."

More cautious now, he motions to my plate. "So eat."

"Alone."

The place is silent.

His friends are watching us.

The old man in the corner, Alice, and the guys in the kitchen, are watching us.

Grey Eyes feels them, too.

The air is thicker than his neck, and that's saying a lot.

Maintaining eye contact, he calls over his broad shoulder, "Alice. Bring my food over here when it comes out."

I almost smile at him calling her that. *Almost.*

Amusement dances in his eyes, like we're in on the fun together now. I'm standing by the booth, wondering what the best course of action is.

If he had a bully vibe, I'd be outta here, but he's got this weird kind of friendly manner that doesn't match that patch and leather.

He leans back and throws an arm over the booth. "We don't have to talk," he calmly says. "I'll even BUY your...salt fest."

Again, I almost smile at his noticing I have a thing for flavor.

Fuck it.

Dropping my backpack on the booth with a loud thump, I sit. "Fine. You're buying. But I'm not giving you anything for it."

"Yeah, pretty much got that," he smirks. To the diner he loudly calls out, "Show's over," and the sounds of normalcy resume.

In a voice tainted with sarcasm and low enough that only he can hear me, I ask the cocky fuck, "You always get what you want?"

Without missing a beat, he throws back in the same hushed volume, "Only if I want it bad enough."

We stare at each other until I volley back, "Well, I hope I don't fall into that category."

His smirk deepens. "I'm just havin' breakfast and I like to look at a pretty face sometimes. I get tired of lookin' at them." He jabs a thumb toward his club then leans in. "Who says I want you, Sunshine?"

I blink at the name, knowing he means it ironically. Leaning in, too, I hold his eyes.

"Most men do."

I stretch and arch my back on purpose.

He's not the only one with an impressive chest.

His eyes fall where I expect them to go, to my cleavage made deep by double D's I inherited from my mother. I've been told I could be Penelope Cruz's sister, and I can see where they get that idea. My mother looked a lot like her, much more so than I.

Only *her* beauty led to her undoing. I won't let that happen to me. I won't be used. For sex. For money. For money for sex.

Not like she was.

But I will manipulate the fuck out of who I want to, if it entertains me...like right now.

Grey Eyes slowly lifts his eyes from my display and there's a gleam there that's not just sexual as he chuckles under his breath and shakes his head. He's not some animal, a dog in heat, or some kid. Like I sensed, he's no rapist or scuzbag. He thinks I'm entertaining, too, and he's having fun with this.

He thinks he found a good opponent.

Smirking back at him, I dig in. Damn, food tastes so good when you're really, REALLY hungry.

The waitress drops his plate down and coldly informs him, "My name's not Alice."

He gives her a wink and a disarming smile. "It is now."

I watch her cold expression melt into confusion.

I know the feeling.

He and I eat in silence, watching each other from time to time. I catch him glancing to my breasts just once. Each time our eyes meet, I hold his look for a moment and then go back to my meal. The residue of these exchanges builds a solid zing in my bloodstream.

Best scrambled eggs I've had in a while.

As I nibble and savor the final sliver of crispy bacon, Grey Eyes spreads strawberry jam on toast and looks at me with caution like he knows the end is coming.

"Why do I get the feeling you're treating me like a bird you don't want to scare off?"

In the same private volume I used, he answers, "Because you're perceptive." After a charged pause where neither of us can look away, he whispers, "I'd say more *cat* than bird. You've got secrets, Sunshine. I like that."

How the fuck can he tell that just by looking at me?

"It was uncomfortable meeting you." I grab my pack, take one last sip of coffee, then get out of the booth and walk away.

It's been a long time since a man woke my body up this way. I am damp and ready for things I don't have time for.

Don't look back, Luna.

Don't do it.

But I can't help myself.

Stealing a glance behind me, I discover him turned around in the booth, unashamedly watching me leave.

Those amazing eyes of his lazily drift up from checking out my ass, and the look in them pulses a response back from my poor, neglected pussy.

I'm almost to the door when I loudly tell him, and the whole diner, "Never gonna happen!"

The cocky fuck *smiles*.

JETT

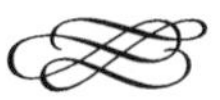

As I stroll back to the Ciphers, Scratch informs me as if I don't already know, "That body would drop any man to his knees."

I give his shoulder a solid smack. "I know it's tough but keep your eyes off her. She's mine."

Honey Badger chuckles deep and rumbly as all four of them watch me head out the door to chase her down. I'm not letting a woman like that get away until I'm done with her.

Squinting against the Southern California sun, I search for the feral beauty. The parking lot has the same unimpressive cars in it as when we rode up.

Out of habit, I do a quick scan of our Harleys as I pass them for the sidewalk, to make sure no one's been dumb enough to fuck with 'em. No sign they've been touched. So I stroll past purple Bougainvillea bushes growing up a fence on the property behind the diner, and discover gold.

There she is walking up Coldwater Canyon.

Her sweet, round ass is ticking from side to side as though to say time is running out, buddy.

She made some distance. On foot. So she doesn't have a car.

I've got a ride I can give her.

"Hey!" I shout up the street. Her shoulders stiffen, but she doesn't slow down.

She's gonna make me chase her.

That I can do.

My boots hit the ground heavily as I break into a run. I don't slow until I've reached her side.

"You're wasting your time," she growls.

"What's your name?"

Silence.

We walk a ways longer, toward Moorpark. There's an Arco on the left and I make mental note, checking my memory for when we gassed up last. It was in Pomona. We're still good.

Since she hasn't given me her name, I offer mine. "I'm Jett."

"Good for you."

Chuckling, I run in front to make her stop walking.

Truth is, I shouldn't be messin' with this kitty.

We came for a dangerous and tricky job.

But we don't back down. Ever.

So now I've got *two* missions, and one is staring at me with fiery deep brown eyes in caramel skin, with lips I need to feel on me in so many places.

She runs a hand through long black locks. She smells dusty – the shampoo smell faded days ago.

So...she probably doesn't live nearby.

Not with how dirty she looks.

What's her story?

I bet her pussy tastes nice and ripe. I don't mind that at all. I love all the flavors.

"Look buddy," she snarls, and means it. "The only reason you don't have your balls kicked into your neck is because you lack the rapist vibe. But 'persistent prick' will get you there, too, if you don't let me pass. This warning is me being nice."

She's got no accent. If I hadn't heard her speak ever, I'd have guessed she's from Mexico, Guatemala, or maybe even Cuba. You never know in L.A.

"Gimme your number and I'll be on my way."

"That smile of yours..." she mutters, irritated as shit. "...tells me you think this tactic is going to work. It won't."

Someone honks at her from a passing Buick and makes sloppy kissy sounds.

"Fuck you!" she calls to the taillights.

I watch the car leaving. See the hand waving out the window. My eyes land back on her tight-lipped expression. It's gotta be a pain in the ass being this beautiful when there's a world full of cocks who'd love to dive into you. That those douche bags honked with *me* here, wearing this patch and clearly not someone you'd fuck with, says it all about her. If they weren't protected by moving metal, they wouldn't try that shit right now.

But she *inspired* them to do it.

They practically couldn't help themselves and took a chance, knowing I couldn't chase them down.

This gives me insight into what she deals with daily. Which means she's right. This tactic ain't gonna fly.

I walk closer to her, changing my tone to a more intimate one, friendlier and less asshole-who-gets-a-ton-of-ass. I don't want to scare her away and I just realized I was about to.

Fuck, we guys sure can be stupid.

"Sunshine, forgive me. I was being a dick. I won't force myself on you." I lean in really close to her. A few more inches and we'd be kissing. The feral beauty holds her breath, dark eyes searching mine like she's confused why she's not punching me. "You don't want to tell me your name, you don't have to." Without warning, I kiss her nose and smile, "I'm sure I'll see you again," right before heading off, back to the diner.

"No..." I turn around. She's looking over her shoulder at me, holding the strap of that beat up backpack. "You won't."

I feel like I'm standing on a cliff, that moment where you decide if you're jumping, or if the mountain will make the decision for you.

She heads away. I turn around and walk off, too, to meet her chess move and see if she's bluffing. I keep expecting the sound of footsteps, or a shout of my name, if she even remembers it.

My chest tightens as the distance grows between us.

Those footsteps never come.

I may see her.

I may not.

The odds aren't in our favor.

Fuse, Scratch, Honey Badger and Tonk are all strapping on their helmets and looking for an answer to what happened on my end.

"Next move?" I ask Scratch, changing the subject.

Our salt and pepper-haired MC Vice President

smacks my shoulder as hard as I smacked his in the diner and announces, "Motel, *Striker*."

I pull my keys out with the chain that keeps them attached to my faded blue jeans. My head is still on the girl. I'm only half paying attention when I mutter, "Striker?"

Fuse laughs and shakes out his longish hair before he straps on his helmet.

I don't like the sound of that laugh. "What? What am I missing here?" I ask him, then look around at all their amused faces.

Tonk's not sure if he should be the one to spell it out for me, since I give him so much shit all the time. He decides to be brave. "You struck out, Jett."

"*Striker*," Fuse chuckles. "It might stick."

Grinning, I mount my bike, feeling the warmth of a sun-heated seat on my balls. "Fuck you guys."

"She was worth the try," Honey Badger laughs, his large belly bouncing as he jumps on his ride. His little helmet on that big head and body is always an interesting contrast, but no one would ever say that aloud. Despite his rotund appearance, Honey Badger earned that name. He can be vicious. Not with *us*. But we don't get on his bad side...like pointing out how he should get a bigger helmet.

"We're only gonna be here a couple nights,"

Scratch tells me from his hog. "That woman? She's the type who'd make you stick around."

"Let's drop it. We've got better things to do."

"Keep tellin' yourself that," Fuse laughs.

I shake my head at his joke and turn on the ignition.

The roar of our engines harmonize, and one after the other, we cruise up Ventura Boulevard, away from Coldwater in search of our next temporary home. We never stay at the same place when we visit a city for a second, third or fourth time, unless there's only that one option. Definitely not the case in a metropolitan city like this one.

In Sherman Oaks, mere blocks west of where we ate, Scratch pulls into a motel that's cleaner than any you'd find in those forgotten towns along lonely highways.

"I can use a good shower," I tell my chosen brothers as the engines die, thinking it'll be a cold one with that feral pussy still on my mind.

Scratch announces to the group. "With what we're about to face, you're all gonna need more than that."

LUNA

Shoving the photograph into the girl's terrified face, I keep my voice hushed, as I demand, "Where is he? You recognize him! I can see the fear in your eyes!"

She's fragile, just like they all are when they've been with him too long. "No!" she insists, shaking her head with big brown eyes darting back the way she came.

In the kitchen on the opposite side of this door are the distinctive sounds of men and women cooking a feast for one of the busiest restaurants in Sherman Oaks.

Everyone talks about Beverly Hills and Bel Air. Yeah, there are powerful people there. Wealth that would make you shit yourself if you found out how much.

But *this* city, Sherman Oaks, tucked into the valley-side of the mountain, is filled with money and power unnoticed. It's less obvious — therefore the perfect place to hide.

But I found him.

He's here.

Not in this restaurant even though he owns it. But he lives not far from where I stand. I can almost smell the rank odor of his cologne, I'm so close.

Standing here in the tiny section that separates the back alley door and the rear entrance to the kitchen, I pull out my gun and point it at her. "No more lies. Do I look like a patient woman to you?"

Trembling, she levels me with a stare that sends shivers into my bones. "If he knew I told you, he would do worse. Kill me. Please kill me! It's my only way out."

I blink in horror because I recognize what I saw in my mother's eyes when I was just a child. It's as familiar to me as cookies and bedtime stories are to someone else more fortunate than I.

Releasing overwhelming pain from my lungs, I lower the gun. "If you tell me, I *will* kill him. You'll never have to be afraid again."

She crumbles. "Where would I go? I don't know anyone. I have no one."

"You'd find a way." I steal a quick glance through

the kitchen door window to make sure no one's coming yet. "*You're a woman.* It's in your blood to be strong. You can handle more than you think. We all can. We have for centuries. Now tell me where he is."

A click happens behind those scared eyes of hers. I see it. She heard me and while her tortured, captive mind doesn't believe me, there's a sliver in her soul that knows what I said is true.

She whispers an address and my eyes close with relief.

"Are you going to warn him I'm coming?"

"He'd know I told you!"

I stop her from explaining more by biting off her next sentence. "Good! Don't. I want it to be a surprise. I'll keep my promise. You'll be free soon. You all will."

An eruption of unusual noises comes from the kitchen. Through a window I see one of the cooks go flying.

"He's here!" The girl clutches my hip as though she is my child.

I aim my gun at the door and attempt to see more from this vantage point.

Why would he destroy his own place with a restaurant full of upper-class witnesses? Some of the wealthiest and well-connected people in town?

It doesn't make sense.

Another cook flies by. There's tons of shouting and

grunts of pain. Unmistakable struggle and fighting. Someone screams. Two men walk past the window.

At the unexpected sight of them I mutter, "What the hell?" edging closer for a better look, with the girl still clinging to me.

Another Cipher jacket almost passes, but stops and blocks my view as the tall, young one shouts to his buddies. "THE COPS!"

Suddenly I hear them, too – blaring sirens in the distance, approaching fast.

I don't know what The Ciphers are doing here, but I can't let these guys see me.

Now that I know where the sadist motherfucker is, I won't let anything take me off course.

I whisper to the girl. "Run!"

"Where will I go?!"

In a different world I'd tell her, *to the police – they're coming. Run to them!*

But I know what *he's* said to her. I know because of his lies, she doesn't trust cops.

I know all too well the false stories he embeds in the women's brains to hold them hostage and impotent.

It's how he keeps his anonymity, and how he gets away with everything – by his victims' willing silence.

Pushing her off me, I insist, "Anywhere is better than where you've been. Go!"

She scurries out the back door into the dark alley.

I step back as the young Cipher lunges forward and punches a hired thug who came to fight. Stunned and wondering, *what the hell*...I step up for a better look.

There's Grey Eyes in the distance, hammering a man in all black, with steady, experienced fists. He looks trained. There is nothing sloppy about those punches – every one hits the target swiftly and to knockout.

There is food everywhere – on the floor, on hanging pots, on shelves. A female chef in all white is huddled in the corner. From her expression, she has no idea what's going on.

She's not alone there.

What the fuck is this gang doing here?

Grey Eyes turns to pull someone off the older Cipher.

He yanks the guy back then looks right into my eyes.

"Fuck!" I gasp, making a break for the door. As the warm night air hits my face I start running.

"Hey!" I hear him call from behind me.

The gun is swinging in my hand.

Fucking RUN, Luna!!

Sirens grow louder in the distance.

RUN!

I turn left and race into the residential street just behind Ventura Boulevard.

RUN!

Shoving my weapon into my backpack while I sprint is one of the most awkward things I've ever done.

Panting I steal a freaked-out glance over my shoulder.

He's not there.

The perfectly groomed landscape is lit only by dim street-lamps. It's supposed to be charming, but there's never been a more terrifying sight when you're this out of place, and in the mindset I'm in.

I have no idea where he went – he could be anywhere – and the sirens are coming closer.

I'm trying to be as quiet as I can by running on grass when it's available. I don't want someone to see me from their suburban window and make that 911 call.

My chest nearly catches fire as a cacophony of motorcycles explodes behind me.

"Shit!" I hiss.

The Ciphers catch up to me in 1.3 seconds flat.

Grey Eyes hits the brakes hard. "GET ON!"

Panting, I look at the upheaval behind us.

"Get the fuck on the bike!" he commands me.

His friends stopped with him, but now they're

taking off, leaving ominous words floating in their wakes...

"They're coming." "Leave her."

Grey Eyes revs the engine.

I see a tan curtain open in the house behind him.

That's all I need to decide. Rushing forward, I grab his bicep and leap onto the back of his Harley.

My backpack feels like it's going to rip my shoulders off as he guns the engine so hard the front wheel comes off the pavement before it lands with a slam and drives into the night.

I wrap my arms around his rock hard torso, clutching abs in one hand and chest in the other.

A master of his machine, the blonde Cipher growls, "Hold on!"

Fucking hell. This street is littered with long, low speed bumps put in by rich people to discourage cruising of their precious neighborhood. Each one is painful until I realize that Grey Eyes rises up off the seat to weather each blow. Learning quickly, I follow suit.

As we chase after the ghostlike taillights of the bikes ahead, we rise up with each bump as though we're one person. With me wrapped around him like this, my thighs around his, I can't help but become aroused.

Mortified, I swallow hard against the sensations

charging powerfully through my body as the bastard gains speed.

At this rate, with my adrenaline rocketing to dangerous heights, this is one hell of a fucking rush.

The tingles become deliriously strong when my pussy hits the vibrating seat, each and every time after we rise to avoid a speed bump. I can't admit to myself that I'm starting to look forward to them.

I clutch his massive body tighter against me, pressing my breasts into the patch on his leather jacket, lying to myself that it's only so I won't fall.

When the sirens become a memory and the bumps are no longer, I try to loosen my hold...but I just can't.

My veins are on fire.

I have no idea where he's taking me.

But I tell myself it's okay, because if he was fighting the men who worked for that motherfucking sadist, I have to know why.

JETT

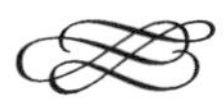

This is the biggest rush. She's riding the back of my baby like she was born to do it. Her huge tits, pressed into my jacket, are driving me insane. My rod is hard, twitching with lust to explore, who is she?

What the hell was she doing there?

Is she one of the women we're supposed to save?

That gun didn't look like a victim to me.

As she clutches onto me her fingers start to search my muscles. She's checking me out, enjoying them, but doing it really slowly like I might not notice. Oh, I notice. As the hand she's got on my abs moves down a little, my cock aches painfully against my zipper.

I'm biting my lip hard.

I want to fuck this chick so badly I can taste her cunt from here.

When I ride up, The Ciphers are clearing out their rooms, exactly as I expected.

The nameless enigma climbs off my bike and I throw my legs over and adjust my crotch right in front of her.

Gorgeous, deep brown eyes dart to my aching bulge, and I nod and mutter, "No fuckin' hidin' this, and I ain't apologizin' for it. But you're safe with me. So come on."

"Where?" she demands as she jogs up.

Under my breath so no witnesses hear me, I inform the gorgeous kitty, "Another motel."

She stops walking. I flip around, not about to take my luxurious time. We have to get out of here. NOW. But she cuts me off before I have a chance to say anything. "What were you doing over there?!"

"I wanna ask you the same thing, Sunshine. Come on. We'll talk later."

I expect an argument, but she follows me. I have a feeling she's used to running, too. She gets that time is of the essence when the police are on your tail.

In my room, I grab the shit I left behind before I go for her arm and speed us both out of here.

"You don't have to drag me!"

Tonk appears outside his room. The others are already climbing back on their bikes.

Scratch throws me his extra helmet and I hand it to her.

"Tell her she's safe."

Honey Badger mutters, "I don't lie to people."

Chuckling, I say, "Fuck you. Thanks a lot."

He locks eyes with the cat and says with complete sobriety, "You're safer with us than with anyone you ever met."

Prideful I glance to her. She locks eyes with each of the Ciphers.

They nod. Nothing big. Just one somber motion each, of agreement, one after the other.

"Fine," she huffs.

I throw my leg over my Harley and wait for her to mount it. As sensually as if she were climbing onto my cock, she gets on, then tugs her helmet strap into place before she wraps those soft, feminine arms around my body again just in time for us to explode out of the parking lot.

This is why we pay cash, and why we stay in motels. Hotels want a credit card and with what we do, we can't leave tracks.

Further into the valley is safe. It's the forgotten land. All the signs are in Spanish. Residential streets are kept nice by the occupants, alone. The businesses are the opposite. They're rundown, graffiti-covered, bar-protected pieces of crap. No corporate or government money comes to take care of the place or the people. They got here, they crossed the border, now they have to fend for themselves.

And I get it.

But when you see it in person, it's a shitty sight.

The dive we pull into makes the place we just left look like luxury. But we all know the truth. No one will bother us here. And the cops wouldn't look for white guys in 'Little Mexico.'

The parking lot is in the back. Perfect. Only one car in it and it probably belongs to the jerk behind the counter. I don't even have to meet him to know what he's like. They're all the same in places like this. It's a rare exception when you find one not watching an old television set, no smile on their faces for years.

Scratch orders Tonk, "Go get the rooms. You're the least bloody."

"Pussy," Honey Badger calls after our youngest and tallest member.

Tonk throws up a middle finger.

"At least his sense of humor is improving," Fuse says under his breath.

The cat shuffles her feet while we're waiting. We all act like it's totally normal for her to be here. No one looks at her. It's like she's invisible, just like you'd do with a feral cat you hope to gain the trust of. We don't want to scare her off until we get answers.

We all asked the same question — why was she there, and with a gun — as we took off in the direction she went, after I spotted her and told them.

Tonk returns and plants a key in each of our waiting palms. He hands me a fresh blanket that's folded and smells of detergent. "For the lady."

With wariness, Scratch mumbles, "Check the mattresses."

Crossing her arms over those sweet tits, the cat growls, "For the lady? I'm not staying the night!"

I smirk at her. "He meant me."

Her face dissolves into confusion at the joke. On a low chuckle I turn my back on her to share a look with Scratch. The crinkles of time deepen around his eyes and, without saying anything aloud, he lets me know this battle will be uphill.

I've gotta admit, if I can talk her into dirtying up this blanket, I wouldn't mind that one bit.

"Why do we have to check the mattresses?" she asks, as she follows me.

As I unlock the grimy door, I answer, "Bed bugs."

Her lips tighten on a grimace, but it doesn't mar that stunning face. She's exotic. A firecracker. And I wanna feel her from the inside.

From the room to my right, Fuse pokes his head out, the first to report his findings. "All clean...ish."

"Well, that's a fuckin' miracle," Honey Badger says, ambling into his room on the other side of Fuse's.

We all confirm the same, then like a bad drum solo, the doors close.

Now it's just me and the kitty.

I lay the blanket on top of the bed and pat it. "Take a load off."

"I'm fine by the door."

Peeling my jacket from my body, I wince a little at the pain in my ribs. That big fucker got a couple in. Just bruises. I check around with my fingers to make sure nothing's broken and as I do the room crackles with sexual chemistry. My veins are racing having her alone in here with just me.

It's all I can do to bide my time so she learns to trust me.

What I *want* is to lift those sweet thighs up and give that feral cunt a nice, long taste.

As I look up to find her full lips parted and slightly moist, my cock twitches. She was carefully watching me inspect my ribcage through this shirt, and she must have fucking licked her lips in the process, which is hot. Very hot. She wants me as badly as I want her. I can feel it, electric in the air.

But I need to be real careful.

She already taught me she's a runner.

I want her to fill me in on who she is before I show her who I can be for her...the greatest fuck of her life.

I consider what I should say next, and opt for trying to amuse her. "You like that?"

She stares for a second like she didn't know I spoke. "Umm...what?"

"Me feelin' my chest like this." I pull up my shirt a little to expose my abs, and feel around, glancing from my naked muscles to her. "You like that?"

Her jaw ticks. "Nope. I was only watching because your knuckles are bloody, that's all."

"Nah. You were lookin' at these." I flex, cocking an eyebrow at her.

She shakes her head like she thinks I'm an asshole.

But I could swear I saw the hint of a smile in her beautiful eyes.

Leaning against the door with a thud, she announces, "Don't fool yourself. I wasn't."

My gaze instinctively drops to her bouncing breasts. She's got a light jacket on. A black one that matches her hair and makes her eyes and teeth look super white.

The backpack is on the floor.

I'm assuming that's where she put the gun.

LUNA

I don't know if this rough-looking guy is being a fucking goofball, or if he really knows how hot he is. He's already proved himself to be a jokester.

He probably knows.

He's not shy, sheepish, or hesitant.

Every move Grey Eyes makes is strong, confident, and careful.

He's playing me, hoping I don't catch on...or mind. I have no idea how I feel, except hot and bothered. Torn, too. I should be checking out the address that girl gave me, but here I am playing games with a biker, telling myself it matters why he and his buddies turned that place upside down.

The only thing that matters is killing *him*. I've waited my whole life for this.

So why am I still here with *this* guy.

His smirk is casual but potent as Grey Eyes heads to the bathroom to wash the blood from his hands. He walks the way only some guys do, like his dick is so big his legs have to shoot out to the sides to make room for the journey. Fucking hot.

I was totally checking him out when he called me on it.

We both know it.

I am so wet right now I'm afraid it'll start to show soon. I should probably excuse myself to the bathroom to do something about it, but I have to wait until he gets out here...and if I lock myself in there, I'll probably end up touching myself to ease this throbbing ache.

I want this guy.

I want his cock.

I want his weight on me.

I want to see if he's the type who'd throw me around like a rag doll and fuck the shit out of me until I can't even remember who I am.

"What's your name?" he calls from where I can't see him. That deep rasp is killing me. I almost walk over, but catch myself and push harder into the door, right by my hidden 9mm.

"What does it matter?" I call back, low and husky. Shit, I can hear the sex in my voice. If I can, he can.

He laughs under his breath. The sound of faucet water stops abruptly and he reappears, this time completely missing the shirt. Half-naked. Jeez.

What a manipulative fuck this guy is.

A thorny tattoo with a C centered beneath it dances on his chest muscles as they tighten and release many times while he dries his hands with the cheap hand towel. He throws me a devilish grin and pokes at his rib, glancing down before looking up from under blonde eyebrows.

Is his pubic hair blonde, too?

Keep your mind in check, Luna.

"Not broken after all," he announces, tossing the towel on a light brown dresser with the top drawer opened slightly. I glance to it and see the corners of a Bible.

"You needed your shirt off to check."

"Yup."

"Makes total sense."

He grins, and it grows into a laugh. "Fuck, you're somethin.' You really are candy for the eyes." Like he means it, his drifting, lingering gaze eats me alive, working slowly down my body and leaving a goose-bump-wake.

"Stop eye-fucking me without my consent."

His eyes shoot up to meet mine. I love that I made him lose that smirk.

"*Why* were you there tonight," I demand.

He blinks at me on a long frown. Shoving his hands in the pockets of faded blue jeans, his belt dips down a little. The tips of a tattoo become visible, but I ignore it.

I'm here for a purpose, and finding the meaning behind a hot biker's tats isn't it.

His chatty charm is gone now.

I really shut him down. Which is fine. Maybe now I'll get answers and I can get the hell out of here.

Observing me from a distance, he growls, "I was gonna ask you the same thing."

"I'm not telling you."

"Then why should I tell you?" he shoots back.

The next exchange is even quicker, each sentence more rapid fire than the last. As this goes on, Grey Eyes walks closer to me.

"Why were you fighting those men?"

"Why were you hiding?"

"Did you follow me?"

"No."

"Yes, you did."

"*After,* yes. Before, no."

"Were you looking for someone in particular?"

"Were you?"

"It doesn't matter what I was doing."

"If you don't tell me, why should I tell you?"

"Because I need to know!"

"And I don't?"

"Did someone hire you?"

"Nope. We work for no master."

This makes me pause. He takes a step closer. I stiffen and press my back harder against the door. His eyes pierce mine like he can read inside my mind or something. Hell, I don't think he's blinked once.

"Neither do I," I breathe as he leans deeper in. Grey Eyes is so dangerously close to my mouth that I can feel his heat.

"Neither do you what?"

"Have a master." *I could use a good fuck, though.* "And I don't want one, either."

"Every woman wants a master."

"Not true," I whisper, fighting him because I'm stubborn but inwardly knowing he doesn't mean equality. He means in the sack. And he's right.

"Deep, deeeeeeep down, she does want a master, Sunshine. She *wants* him to take charge. Make her pant his *name* as she quivers underneath him."

With his eyes all hooded and his naked chest lightly touching the tips of my breasts through my jacket and shirt, Grey Eyes lowers his hand. I follow it, unable not to look. He hovers thick, calloused fingers from riding, just short of my jeans' zipper and crooks his middle finger as though it were about to be inside me. He's almost touching me there. I've stopped breathing.

With a low, slow rasp, he continues to tease me as we both stare at those fucking fingers of his. "*Every* woman wants a *real* man. One who knows how to touch her...here. And that man, Sunshine, *that* man she'd call Master."

His eyes crawl up my body, locking with mine as I press the back of my head into the door, wishing he'd touch me so I could punch him. Or grab the back of his head and eat him alive. Whichever came first.

"Baby," he murmurs, "...this is a fucked-up situation. I want you. But I'd never take you against your will." He kisses my nose like he did this morning, but this time real slow. "However...if you *gave* yourself to me, you'd thank me for it."

He leans in to kiss me but drops down without doing so, grabs my backpack and flashes away from me, pulling my gun out.

I explode, "What the fuck!?" pushing off the door and coming at him. "Give me that!"

He jumps on the bed and holds it up. "Now what's this for, huh?"

"You tricked me!"

"Yup."

I chase him around the bed, totally helpless. I'm

not about to tackle him outright. That weapon is fucking loaded.

"GIVE IT BACK!"

He grins. "You sound like my brother Jeremy when I found a love letter from his ex-girlfriend! Now, now, Sunshine, stop trying to grab me. You said it was never gonna happen. Can't change your mind just because I got ya all wet, baby."

"FUCK YOU!"

Waving my gun at the ceiling, he laughs loudly then cocks an eyebrow, "Well, if you insist."

"It wasn't an offer!"

"Sounded more like an order."

Growling, I back away and cross my arms. "You really don't want to get on my bad side."

His eyes dance and he tucks the gun in the back of his beltline. Throwing his gorgeous arms out wide, his naked, stunning chest is on full display. The hair under his arms is blonde, and that means...*Stop it, Luna!!*

"I'll tell ya what, Kitty, you tell me what your name is, and why you were there, and I just might give you back your piece."

"What's YOUR name?"

"I already told you, Sunshine. It's Jett. Jett Cocker. Very fun meeting you. Your turn."

Wickedly, I smile. "Oh right. You did mention your name. I just forgot, because I don't give a shit."

His grin falters, but then expands. "Ooooooweeeeee! You are a fuckin' spitfire! I love this!"

I dryly announce, "That wasn't the reaction I was aiming for."

Jett reaches up and holds onto the popcorn ceiling. He looks massive, a fucking monster of a man. If it weren't for that smile I would be a little scared, but surprisingly, I'm not.

I am just pissed off and *maybe* enjoying it.

"What's your name, Sweetheart?"

"Kitty. Baby. Sweetheart. Sunshine. Any of those work fine, thanks."

"Alright, SMARTASS, what were you doin' hidin' outside that kitchen with a gun in your pretty little hand?"

He pauses, waiting for me to reply.

I say nothing, smirking back at him.

His eyes narrow as he sizes me up. "Because I'm thinkin' that you aren't involved in the Human Trafficking thing. You're not the *victim* type."

Unexpected pain punches me in the chest as I see my mother's face.

Suddenly I can't breathe.

I turn away so he can't see that my whole world just came to a complete stop.

The room goes dead quiet.

LUNA

He jumps off the bed and lands with a thud on the aged carpet.

A second later I feel his hands softly touch my elbows as he whispers, "Hey, I'm sorry...I didn't know."

I was having fun and now it's ended with the reminder of where I come from and what I've lived through. The little girl in me wants to lean into his strength. It's a foreign desire. I've never turned to men for comfort. They are always the enemy.

But his voice. It's so...compassionate. I never hear that tone. Especially not in my own head.

Before I know what I'm doing, I let him wrap his arms around me. He rests his forehead on the back of my head.

A scared little girl inside me whispers, *'Can we stay like this forever?'*

And because I don't understand these feelings at all, I turn around to look into his eyes, searching them and wondering where my voice has gone.

Grey Eyes stares into me like he can handle this.

Are these tears tugging inside of me? I haven't cried in years!

Over a throat dryer than I've ever had, I rasp, "I don't need to be held."

He nods and murmurs, "No, you're too strong for that."

"That's right," I whisper, barely able to talk.

"C'mere." He pulls me in against his strength and hugs me so hard it almost hurts. "I don't know what happened to you, Sunshine," he whispers against my hair, "but I'm sorry it did. I wish I could make it go away."

Oh God. Why'd that stab me in the heart so deeply? Fuck. I can't...I just can't...hold back.

I rise on my tiptoes. Sensing what I need, he leans down to meet me, staring into my eyes for a split second before devouring me in a kiss. His jaw unlocks and Grey Eyes turns me into his clay, molding my lips with his, seeking out my tongue and teasing it until I can't help but moan. There's so much pain in the sound. I heard it, and it only deepens my agony.

"Sunshine..." he murmurs against open, waiting lips. We lock eyes as he asks me silent questions, his eyelids heavy with hunger.

He lifts me up by my thighs and wraps my trembling legs around his body right here where he stands. As we eat each other alive he rushes us to the nearest wall and throws us against it, groaning as his hot bulge pushes into the crotch of my jeans. I can't get enough of these kisses. He's so good at them.

"*Fuck,*" he growls into my mouth.

"Uh huh," I moan, opening moist lips even more to invite his skilled tongue to claim mine again.

I need to taste him.

I need to be tasted.

I need this.

As our lips lock once more, tongues lashing and teasing, my stomach clenches. Heat rushes through me. He grinds his need into mine. Thick fingers yank my shirt off, snapping my bra and throwing it aside while he groans at my naked, full breasts.

Being stared at like this is distracting and I feel the pain drift in again, but the sexy bastard grinds his angry bulge against me really hard and makes me forget anything except for how much I need his cock inside me. NOW.

"I am going to fuck the shit out of you, Sunshine," he growls, devouring my mounds with hot kisses, kneading my ass with strong hands. "Are you ready for this?"

I moan, "Uh huh..." as I watch him chewing on me, turning my nipples into tight pebbles until I'm gasping and starving to feel all of his length. He groans deep and gutturally when I whisper, "That feels so gooooood."

"Let's do this, baby," We propel off the wall and careen to the bed where we fall like a chopped down tree, caving the mattress with his weight on mine. I'm crushed beneath his muscles. It's perfect. It's heaven. As I'm panting and holding my breasts, he yanks off our pants, watching what I'm doing, how much touching myself in front of him is turning me on.

"Holy fuck, whoever you are, you're gorgeous."

His boxer briefs are obscene, the tent massive.

I can't wait to feel that cock tear into me.

It's been so long since I've been fucked. And I've never in my whole life been kissed the way this man just kissed me.

"Come on!!!" I moan, writhing on the bed. "What are you waiting for?"

He steps back and runs both hands through his hair like he can't believe this is happening. His deep rasp sends shivers into my blood as he growls, "I'm done waiting." He dives onto me, pulling me up to devour me. I melt in his arms and respond unashamedly.

"Show me," I whisper as my pussy clenches, so excited about what she's about to receive.

Shoving his hand down he produces a cock so enormous it makes my back arch, the response instinctual and instantaneous.

He's hung like crazy.

Wide girth.

Terrifying length.

And there's that tattoo I spied.

Tear 'em Down To Stand 'em Up.

"What does that mean?" I whisper.

He glances down for a split second like he has no idea what I'm talking about, and then locks on me again. "Our code."

Grey Eyes crawls onto me panther-style, and lifts me up by my ass without hesitation, burying his face in my pussy until I am screaming, "HOLY FUCK! OH MY GOD!" He's licking me, using his fingers, flicking my clit like a pro. All of it is crushing me into dust.

He rumbles into my sopping wet pussy, "Cum on my tongue, baby girl. Cum for me." I cry out as he starts pumping those fingers in such a way that I lose my fucking mind. "That's it," he growls. "Cum for me just like this. Yeah, I can feel you cumming now. Ooooh yeah."

Rising up, he kisses his way up my body, cupping my cunt and rubbing it with skill to stretch the orgasm out. "How the fuck do you know how to do that?" I rasp, arching my back as he takes my nipple into his mouth and sucks hard. "GOD!!!!"

"You like that?" he smirks.

"DO I LIKE IT?!!"

Grey Eyes chuckles low and dirty. Gripping both my thighs with confidence, he touches the tip of his cock to my dripping opening. It's half my juices and half his saliva.

"I'm safe," he rasps.

At first I don't know what he means. Then I get it. "Me too. Totally clean."

He kisses me deeply. Suddenly my fingers are laced with his and strung above my head as he begins to enter me, pushing his cock in slowly inch by inch, savoring it as our tongues beat a steady rhythm. "Fuck!" he growls into my mouth as he finishes the distance, thrusting in as deeply as he can get. His fingers are strangling mine, his teeth gnawing their way down my neck as he snarls into my ear, "You're so wet, Sunshine. You feel how slippery this entry was?"

I gasp as he starts to move.

"Harder," I whisper.

"With me, you get what you ask for," he snarls right before he starts pounding the strength of his whole body into and against mine. Letting go of my hands he claws my legs and manipulates my hips to his satisfaction, drinking in my desperate moans until he yells out, grimacing as he holds back his climax. "We're gonna make this last."

I'm taffy in one of those machines. He moves me like I weigh nothing. His cock is so delicious and so fucking hard I can't believe we weren't doing this right on that table at breakfast and every moment since.

He expertly sits us up, puncturing my wet cave again and again as I writhe on top of him and grab a fistful of his hair. "Harder!"

The beast rasps, "YES," right before he chews on my tongue and proceeds to pummel me with jarring beats and without tenderness.

Everything snaps. We are not in control anymore. It's primal and hot as hell. He groans as I bend his head back and kiss him as roughly as he's fucking me right now.

Suddenly we're on the floor. I'm on top and he's pawing my breasts skillfully. I'm riding him without shame as I reach down and grab him by his jaw to demand, "Why does this feel so fucking good?!"

He grins, reaching down and holding his thumb on my clit as I ride his length. Within seconds I'm crying out, cumming again, dripping down his balls. I know because I'm grabbing them and making him yelp.

"You like that?"

"I shouldn't, but I do," he moans, flipping me over and ramming into me with everything he's got. Whimpering and sore, I begin to shake and tremble. "That's right, Sunshine, cum for me again, baby. Cum for me. Fuck, you feel so good I want to join you. But you're not getting off that easy."

"Shit!" I moan, covering my face with my hands as tears slide down. This release has me, and it's everywhere. He sees my tears, dives down to kiss me and I respond like I've never been kissed – rasping his name into his lips until he growls and lifts me off the ground.

We're in the bathroom when the fifth one hits me. He's behind me, and we're both watching us fuck in the mirror.

Lips raw.

Skin Flushed.

Sweat dripping.

I twist my torso for a kiss. Rubbing my breast he latches his mouth onto mine and draws out the hot, tingling burn of multiple contractions with slow sure strokes, knowing how sensitive I am now. As I cum, he growls into my lips, which just drives me further into the pleasure. As soon as I'm boneless, he buries his face in my neck and lifts me up.

In a flash, I'm bent over the only chair in the motel room, a fake leather thing that matches nothing.

"Jett..." I moan over and over as he massages my ass and slowly rides me from behind. His cock is amazing. It feels so good filling me up to completion like this. I cry out, "No fucking way!" as I feel the tremble threaten me one more time. I want to feel *him* cum. I don't want to be the only one. I squeeze the muscles inside my cunt and try to hold it back. With my hair matted with sweat to my cheek, I look over my shoulders and lock eyes with him to shout, "Cum inside me you fucker or I'll slap the shit out of you when this is done!"

He starts laughing, pulls out of me, literally throws me over his shoulder and tosses me onto the bed. I yelp as he dives into me, yanking my hands above my head. Our fingers lace and he moves my thighs open wider, plunging deeply into me. Pulling back from kissing me, his eyes change, something clicks in them. He's looking at me in an intimate way. To someone like me, this is very unnerving. I can't escape his seeing me.

Like, really seeing me.

My chest twists and I look to the side, locking onto the closed curtains instead.

"Don't do that."

"I can't!" I whisper.

"Look at me!"

"No, I can't. It's too much!"

"LOOK. AT. ME." He stops moving and loosens his hold on my hands.

Desperate for it not to end like this, I meet his eyes. My whole body is shaking. I know I must look strange, this terrified of being vulnerable.

Fucking is one thing.

Him making it intimate is another.

He kisses me softly. "Just take the wall down for this one night, Sunshine. Just let the fucker go and enjoy this."

"I don't know how!" I close my eyes and feel his lips touch mine.

He murmurs against them, "Let me show you."

Opening my eyes he gives me this look like I can trust him. Everything I know about men says I can't. But this guy...I nod very slowly and those hips start to fuck me again. We're locked in a visual embrace. Our fingers weave tightly together and he begins to move faster. My head falls back and I gaze and whisper, "Oh God," as tears gather in my eyes.

He nods like it's okay, then kisses me deeply, filling me up the whole time. I feel his cock swell and know this is the moment. He pulls back, gritting his teeth as he stares into my eyes. A deep moan escapes me, one that goes on as he explodes and roars so loudly I know his friends can hear. My body unleashes under his and I cum just as hard as he does. It is unabashed delirium.

He collapses onto my lips, moaning into them as he grinds everything he has to give into my sore little cunt.

"Fuck, Sunshine, holy dammit, FUCK FUCK FUCK!!!!"

I whimper in his arms and kiss his hair as he slumps onto me, slippery with sweat.

In the quiet that follows, I feel peace, crushed beneath him and staring lazily at the ceiling, thinking of him, this and us. Soon I hear the steady breathing of his dozing and I smile, lightly petting his head with my short nails.

My eyes fall on the gun he set on the nightstand, and my smile slowly disappears.

JETT

A knock on my motel door jars me awake. Fuck, I haven't slept like that in...years? Yeah, feels like it's gotta be years. Stretching with my eyes still closed, I shout to whoever is on the other side, "HANG ON!"

Rolling over, I discover I'm alone in the bed.

Sitting up with a start, I scan the room and see the bathroom door shut. Relaxing, I call to her, "Hey Sunshine, you wake up before me?"

The name is ironic. She's a dark girl. Disturbed and tortured by a past I want to know more about.

Rolling off the bed, I trudge over and rap on the door. "Whatever your name is...get on out here. Time for breakfast and you never answered my questions."

No response.

I knock again then try the handle.

It's unlocked and... "Motherfucker!" She's not here.

Whipping around I search for the backpack.

The gun.

The girl.

They're gone.

"FUCK!"

Quick, angry strides get me to the motel room door. Scratch waits on the other side, framed by bright sunlight.

"Did you see her leave?"

He somberly shakes his head. "No, man. I was just comin' to wake you. We've been up for over an hour. You're usually first one up."

Dragging angry fingers through my hair I shout, "SHIT! I CAN'T BELIEVE THIS!"

"She stayed over?"

Honey Badger walks up and before he sees my face, asks, "Did you find out what she was...oh fuck. She took off on you, didn't she?"

Fuse and Tonk walk up behind them. I'm buck-naked. They don't say a word. They just overheard what is going on and there's no way they're gonna fuck with me right now.

Glaring my answer, I snatch up my jeans and snarl, "I need some food."

"A girl ran out on Jett?" Fuse mutters, like he can't believe it.

It's true. I'm normally the one leaving.

Furious and feeling like an absolute fuckin' idiot, I shout, "FUCK THAT. I need to shower first. Get the smell of this bitch off me." Slamming the door, I swear under my breath. In fact, I can't stop swearing.

How'd I sleep through her sneaking out?

Did she drug me?

Nah. I just took my guard down.

This'll teach me never to do that again.

Even after we eat, the air is still stiff. We're sitting around a table at 'Four 'n 20 Restaurant and Pie' on Laurel Canyon when Tonk pulls out a phone and throws it on the table.

"That the one?" Scratch asks, picking it up.

"Yeah."

Shoveling omelet into my mouth, I grumble, "What is it?"

"A burner phone. I grabbed it off one of the guys I knocked out last night," Tonk says.

My eyebrows shoot up.

Tonk's learning.

I grab the phone and say with a full mouth, "Nice work," as I check it out.

As he mops syrup up with a last, lonely waffle chunk, Honey Badger shrugs. "Yeah, but what do we do with it?"

The five of us finish our meal, ruminating over the problem. There are three dialed numbers in its memory, but it's not like we'll be able to find the addresses by Googling these digits. People don't have their addresses on display like that, unless they're totally clueless. Not the case here.

We're not spies. We don't have access to Internet geniuses.

"It's a useless piece of plastic," Scratch grumbles, turning it over in his big paw.

Suddenly I remember my brother. "Give me that. I might have a way." Scratch hands me the thing and I head out to the parking lot, pulling my own phone out and dialing as the warm sun digs into my scalp.

Justin answers on the first ring. "Jett! How the hell are ya? I haven't heard from you in months."

"I'm good. In California."

"No way!" A thunderclap sounds in the background. "Hear that?"

"Fuck, I miss those storms. It's not rainin' where I am. Ever."

He laughs. Justin shares one major thing with our father, he's a politician and well connected with the power players. Only unlike our dad, he plans to be in the Senate. I think he wants to one-up Congressman Michael Cocker, which I wouldn't mind at all. But if I'm honest, Dad would be proud of Justin if he surpassed him in power. It's me he's never proud of. Fuckin' asshole.

"How are ya, Justin?" I glance over to our Harleys, checking them out like I always do. "How's Jason?"

"Why does everyone always ask about my twin? We're not attached," he laughs, adding, "Thank God. You know him, Jett. Forever tangled with some crazy chick. He's got a new girl. Real piece of work. I hate her."

"You hate all Jason's girls."

I can hear by the echo of his laughter that he's in his huge office. It's three hours ahead there, so I might have caught him just before lunch. Good. Need him near his resources, and somewhere private.

"I think you're just jealous, man," I tell him, referring to Jason's women.

Justin laughs again, loud and heartily, like there's no way that's true.

I grin and walk over to my saddlebags, adjusting the strap on one side just because.

"You meet *Jake's* woman yet?" Justin asks.

"Not yet. Heard about her when I saw him in

Colorado though. We talked on the phone a couple months ago, he told me he was pretending to go slowly because she had a problem with his age, still. But then Ma told me it got serious, last time we spoke."

"I'd say so. They're getting married. You should come."

A pang twists my chest up and my smile leaves me flat. Gazing up at the never-ending Southern California sunlight, I mutter, "We'll see."

"Fuck what Dad thinks, Jett. You need to be there. Hang on a second...what?" A woman's muffled voice is in the background. She's saying something official. Justin tells her, "Okay, let him know I'll call him back after I talk to my brother." He returns to me. "You better come, Jett. You'll regret it if you don't."

"I'll be there in spirit."

"You're here in spirit all the time. Try to be here in person for once."

"We'll see."

We're silent a second. I know my younger brother is seriously considering whether or not to try harder, but he knows me too well. "Why'd you call, Jett? I can tell you've got a motive. You sound tense."

"I need to see if you can run some phone numbers for me. I need addresses."

"Hang on...Mary? Will you give me a minute? I'll buzz you when I'm done here." He waits and I hear a door close in the distance. Then another thunderclap. Justin's voice gets lower. "You guys fighting the good fight again?"

"Always."

"Look, I've got some buddies on the force, but finding addresses...I need a reason."

Glancing over, I lock eyes with Scratch through the window. The others are deep in conversation.

"Justin, this one's deep. Not just some gang terrorizing some town. I'm talkin' human trafficking. I don't know how Scratch got the call, but we're about to shut something major down. Only we can't find the guy without your help. This phone might have the answers if it's not too late."

Justin whistles long and low. "Wow. I think you're doing better things than I am."

"When you work outside the law you can get more done."

"Alright, don't say things like that on my cell phone."

I chuckle, "You're too low level for them to be watching. When you reach Senate, I'll send ravens." He laughs, but I hear the tension isn't only in my voice now. "I need this, Justin. There are women involved. We can give them a way out. You can help. That's why you want to be a politician, right?"

"Alright. What are they?"

Going through the burner I give him all the numbers called. There are only three.

"Jett, you know these may not lead anywhere. Where'd you get the phone?"

"We went dancing last night. A gentleman didn't need it anymore, once the music stopped."

He exhales. "Please use code like that from now on. I'm serious. I'm here for you. You know that. But I have a future I'm building. If we're going to...work together...it's gotta be discreet."

"You got it. I appreciate it, Jus."

"I'll tell Jake you're comin' to the wedding."

"Don't you fuckin' dare. Don't tell him that shit."

After silence, he says, "Try to make it."

"I hear you. Say hi to Jason. Tell him I'll call soon."

"I'll tell *everyone* you said hello," he says with meaning.

"Asshole," I laugh, and hang up.

Yeah, tell Dad I said hey. Let's see how riled up he gets when he hears that.

Never got a thank you for what I did for him with Jake.

He can go to hell. Fucking hypocrite.

Nodding to Scratch through the glass, I watch him rise and tell the others to join. They amble out and squint as the sun hits them. That's the darkest diner we've ever been in. Why they want you to start your day in a cave beats me.

"Now we wait," I tell them.

Scratch nods. He's the only one I've shared my family connections with. No one needs to know my dad's up in Washington and my brother's heading there.

The only person Scratch has talked to in my family is my mom. She asked to speak to him when I was on the phone with her early on. Then she went and acted old-school telling our V.P. to watch over her boy. He didn't let me live that down for a long time. But I think he was secretly jealous.

I come from the best family of all the Ciphers I know.

It's not because of my problems with my father that I ride in this club. It's because of the burning itch in my soul, the urge to fight, and for a cause. I'm not the sit in an office, kiss babies type.

Fucking shit up, that's more my life.

I'm suited for it.

We all are.

Fuse asks, "You have some internet nerd in your back pocket?"

I smile at the idea of anyone thinking of Justin as a nerd— he and his identical twin Jason are probably the prettiest of us Cocker Brothers. "Something like that."

Scratch squints at the sky, thinking. After a moment, he grumbles, “Saddle up. Let’s ride.”

“Where?” Tonk asks.

“Anywhere,” Honey Badger tells him, knowing there’s nothing better for us to do while we wait.

Scratch gives me a look and jerks his head away from the others. “Jett, come here.”

We walk to get some privacy.

“You got nothing out of the girl?”

“Not anything we can use.”

He smirks at my joke, but his eyes see more than I want them to. Why’d he have to remind me? For the last half hour I’d managed to forget about her.

An unfamiliar beep goes off on my phone. I frown as I read an alert from my credit card company warning me about an unusually large charge in a new city...this one. We just got here yesterday, and now someone is... What the hell?

“Motherfucker,” I whisper, stunned.

“What?”

“She stole my credit card! What the hell did she buy for almost six hundred dollars at a fuckin’ Bed Bath and Beyond?!”

Scratch makes a hissing sound and cranes over to check out what it says on my outstretched phone. “What the hell...”

“Fucking cunt stole my credit card!”

He sighs like he sees something I don't.

"What, Scratch? What's that face for?"

"You never call women that."

"Well, I just did."

"She got to you."

"SHE DIDN'T FUCKIN' GET TO ME."

I head for my hog.

The other Ciphers look away quickly, except Fuse. He's got a son from a woman who drives him crazy, Melodi. He gives me a look like he gets it. Before I have a chance to tell him to go to hell, he breaks eye contact and flips his ignition on, motor roaring to life.

LUNA

"Mommy, why won't you teach me Spanish?"

My mother lowered her voice to a whisper as she always did when he was in the house. "Because I want you to do something with your life."

My five-year-old brain couldn't understand how learning my mother's native language would hinder that.

"Why would learning Spanish stop me, Mommy?"

Her eyes went sharp then with both anger and pain. She roughly grabbed my arm and whispered, "Luna! The people with power speak ENGLISH. Speaking only Spanish keeps us small. There are no jobs for girls of your skin color if you do not speak English! Do you want to be poor?! Being poor is evil, Luna. It makes bad people prey on you because you are vulnerable. You are meant for bigger things! Do you understand?"

With tears in my eyes I nodded, but I was lying. I didn't really understand.

Not until I was older.

My mother was taught English by my Grandmother, who died before I was conceived. Her father died, too, during a raid on the drug cartel's home where he worked and lived. He was one of the bad guys. Her brother died that day, too. He was her age and trying to be like their father. He died being like him.

Sofia, my mother, was very scared and alone when *he* found her. The men in her life had kept her sheltered, but *he* said he would show her great things, if she'd just trust him.

He was powerful. Charismatic. Educated about life in ways she was not. He told my mother he saw potential in her and offered to smuggle her into America.

He promised to take care of her and the baby who was on the way...me.

But when she got here, she all too quickly discovered what kind of evil he was. And she was told there was no way out. She had no money. No friends. No support.

And she had a baby to house and feed.

He manipulated her mind, but he never killed her spirit.

I was raised in a house of prostitution. I saw things a little girl never should, although the women tried to shield me as much as possible. I didn't know why I was the only child there. Sometimes the women got pregnant but the babies always left. It was just the way things were.

When I was ten years old, my mother's body was dragged out past my door.

At the sight of her bloody corpse, I screamed, *"What happened to my mommy!? Where are you taking her?! Let her go! LET HER GO!!!"*

Her limp, naked legs made a horrible scratching sound on the jagged carpet, and I grabbed onto them so hard the sheet came off. One of his thugs covered her but I'd seen more than I should have.

I completely lost it.

I begged through sobbing screeches, "DON'T TAKE HER FROM ME! MOMMY!!! MOMMY!!" And as they pushed me off and I fell to the ground, I whispered, "Don't leave me here all alone."

One of the other sex-slaves, a woman in her twenties from Guatemala named Louisa, yanked me back and covered my mouth. She'd seen the men begin to get irritated, and she didn't want them to punish me. I was always getting punished, and she knew they wouldn't spare me even that tragic day.

In a stupor, I heard three of the other women whispering in Spanish what had happened to my mother. I couldn't understand them all the way, but I got pieces of what they were saying. And I knew 'muerto' meant dead. I'd heard the word used in that hellhole many times and I knew then that it wasn't a trick. My mother was gone forever.

It was like she never existed.

There was no funeral.

There was no report made to the police.

You can't trust the cops.

They're in on it.

If you run for help, you'll be tortured. Not just sent back to your country...but whipped and beaten until you can never talk again, ever. That's what they'll do to you.

"If I don't find you first."

That is what *he* told my mother. That is what she believed. They all did and still do.

People think human smuggling and trafficking are the same. They're not. Smugglers get you across the border and then you have to find your own way. They don't hold you hostage. They just get you safely here.

Traffickers use people. Make money off them. Hold them hostage with lies and threats, making them sex-slaves, sweatshop workers, sell them for 'marriages,' always convincing them that they can't go to the police. Yes, it goes on here in beautiful and free America. But no one talks about it.

I have never gone to the cops with what I know. Is that because I don't believe they can help me? Partly, yes. But really it's because...they wouldn't let me kill him.

"Luna, I heard what happened to your momma."

Sniffling and terrified of the evil man, I nodded.

In the fireplace behind him, flames licked the air, his imposing profile all the more terrifying to me because of them. He was counting money – cash. Lots and lots of cash. It lay on the table in dirty stacks next to a box with more inside, and his slimy fingers relished the feel of the paper as he picked up each note one by one.

"It's too bad. She was sought after. Beautiful, though time was starting to take a toll on her looks. But you are growing old enough to take her place, so I guess there is no real loss here...is there?"

Images of what the women had to do in this house flashed before grief-stricken ten-year-old eyes as I held my breath in terror.

He smiled hideously. "Your tits are big now, too, just like hers." That I hit puberty at age nine was the sickest joke nature ever played.

On a low, ugly chuckle, he asked himself, "I wonder how much they'd pay for a virgin."

The lump in my throat twisted to coal as I watched pure evil rise from his chair and walk toward me.

Out of instinct I recoiled.

"STAY!" he shouted, as if I were a dog.

Panic-stricken I froze and watched as his wrinkly fingers reached over and slithered across my right breast. He made a noise of appreciation that sounded like a snake smelling its dinner.

Tears started to pour down my cheeks. I made no move to hide them. I wanted my mother. I wanted to be rescued.

Malignant eyes locked on mine and I knew then he was going to rape me. And there was nothing I could do to stop him.

"They'd never know you weren't a virgin...would they?"

"Sir?" a male voice interrupted.

The age-spotted hand retracted as Evil shouted, "I'M BUSY!"

"Two of the girls are missing. The ones we told you about."

I knew immediately he meant Teresa and Juaquina. I'd heard them talking about running away, and because they'd found a friendship in each other, the feat seemed possible. They were new and not beaten down yet.

They thought maybe the rope couldn't really hold them if they pulled it out together.

They talked in front of me the way everyone did, making the mistake of thinking because I was young, I wasn't listening. But I didn't tell anyone what they were planning. I never thought they'd actually try it. They'd be the first. In my mind, it was impossible, leaving here. So I kept my mouth shut and acted like I hadn't heard a word. Didn't even tell my Mom.

Yet here this bodyguard was, saying they'd done it. Something bloomed in my heart I'd never felt before – hope.

Evil was furious. Fire seemed to explode from his eye sockets as he rushed out to drag those poor girls back. Silently I prayed for them to make it and never be found.

And that gave me an idea.

Alone in the room, I raced forward and grabbed the wooden box of money. I shoved the bills he was counting onto the neat stacks inside and ignored the ones that escaped fluttering to the ground like butterflies.

If they wanted to be free, let them.

With everyone distracted looking for those young women...I escaped.

I'm twenty-eight now. Over the eighteen years since, I have imagined his face when he found me gone that night. Was it the next morning? Or did he come home and go to the room my mother and I had shared with five other harrowed women, to grab my arm and drag me to his bed?

Now is the time of reckoning. The girl told me the truth. This mansion is his. I saw a familiar face of a bodyguard in one of the windows as I stole across the lawn. Although he's much older than when I knew him, I'll never forget that profile. It was the man who'd pushed me back when I tried to hold onto my murdered mother for one more precious second.

Evil has profited since I ran away. If this is where he keeps the girls now, he must have more of them and business is booming. I feel sick picturing his gloating face as he dines with his demons night after night on food he'd never serve the women who earned it.

As usual the grounds around the house are unguarded. There are cameras, but few. The people who come here don't want their 'good' names connected to atrocity.

Silently I move toward a side door and pull out the skeleton key I got off a drifter in Miami. It works most of the time. Slipping it into the lock, I hold my breath then turn. It doesn't budge.

Twitching with nervous apprehension, I tuck it

into my pocket and look over to the quiet street. Not a single car has passed. We're high enough in the hills that no one comes through except those who live in this neighborhood. If they only knew what was right next door.

I can't see the van I stole, which means they can't either.

It's late. He'll be in bed by now. Or having cognac by the fire. I've no doubt he'll have a fucking fireplace in his upgraded bedroom.

I will slip in there and shoot him before he even says my name.

Jimmying the door with a paperclip takes longer than the key would have, but I'm a pro. Soon I hear the low click and know I'm almost there. My heart is beating painfully hard. I've waited my whole life for this moment. The knob gives under my pressure and the door opens.

Success.

With the gun in my hand, extra bullets in my jacket pocket, I go in.

What the fuck?

Do ALL the lights have to be on?

Swiftly and carefully I slink forward, listening for voices.

Several men are chatting casually in a room just ahead on the right about Kobe Bryant, obviously fans.

That's right, boys, keep talking sports. Stay nice and distracted. As I near the open door I slow and wait until I gauge the distance from me to them. From the acoustics it's a big room. When I'm satisfied they're not nearby and are engrossed in recounting last night's game, I edge by unseen.

Rooms on my left are closed and quiet. I know he's on the upper floor, where he believes he deserves to be. I'm going to send him underground, back to hell where his vacant soul belongs.

JETT

The plan is simple. We park the bikes far enough away that our arrival isn't broadcasted. We train when we aren't on a mission. We've got guns, but we usually use our hands. The Ciphers don't fuck around with shit like this.

We're amped and ready.

"Holy shit," Tonk mutters under his breath as he catches sight of the mansion. It's something out of a fucking magazine for the wealthy and fucked up. Darker than most on the street. Foreboding as hell.

"Your heart pumping as hard as mine is?" Honey Badger growls.

I reply, "Can't wait," with my eyes on the prize.

Fuse and I exchange a look, too. We're all waiting for Scratch to give the word since it's his job.

He's locked and loaded. "Fuckin' cameras."

Scanning, I spot 'em in the corners plus one pointed at anyone coming up the u-shaped driveway. "You thinkin' what I'm thinkin'?" I ask Scratch.

From the corner of his eyes he looks at me, and nods real slow like. His steady gaze rakes over each of us before he snarls, "Let's do it."

Turning on his heel he heads back the way we came, me on his tail.

The others didn't catch on, but they trust.

At the bikes, Scratch tells them, "Fuck low profiles."

Their eyes gleam with instant comprehension.

Honey Badger smirks, "Give me an explosion over a whisper any day."

Fuse grins and Tonk nods he's ready to go.

In seconds we're on the hogs, guns stuck in our belts, helmets still latched to the rides. With the wind in our hair we roar into action, revving the beasts with everything they've got. Shattering the silence we create a big scene, tearing up the driveway right in full view.

Security lights come to life. Some idiot helps us out by opening the front door as we sprint up the steps, surprised and not ready for this shit.

Honey Badger earns his name yet again by smacking the guy's rifle into the air. The gun goes off.

None of us flinch.

He gives him a swift uppercut punch with his other hand, then using the gun to sucker-punch the fuck in the gut.

One after the other we explode into the mansion, running fast, anticipating a lot more men and a lot more bullets.

I take down a couple guys in black.

My brothers fight at least that many, each.

I hear a shout and look over my shoulder in time to dodge a bullet aimed at my fuckin' head.

I punch the guy senseless.

This goes on until it's quiet.

I scan the wreckage and discover Fuse on the floor, out, blood all over him.

Scratch, panting, sees him at the same time I do.

We rush over to find our friend shot in the shoulder and his nose bloodied up and broken.

Honey Badger is in a room to our left, punching the ever livin' shit out of someone.

Scratch checks Fuse's pulse and slaps his face. "He's not gonna die from a shoulder wound. Fuse! Wake up!"

Groaning, he blinks awake in agony. "FUCK! DON'T SLAP MY FUCKING NOSE!"

"You got shot. You alright?"

"Yeah," he rasps, looking at me like he can't believe he went down.

"We won," I tell him.

Tonk appears from another room down the foyer. "You're never gonna believe this."

"Stay here." Scratch and I rise up to follow our youngest Cipher. Neither of us likes the look on his face.

Are we too late?

"Honey Badger!" Scratch calls into the room where the punches are still comin.' They stop.

"Yeah?"

"Give it a rest."

He appears and follows us. "Motherfucker called me fat."

Cracking my right shoulder back into place, I grin, "Well, he said that to the wrong guy."

"Damn straight," he mutters, still pissed.

With his eyes dead, Tonk growls, "In here."

JETT

We walk inside and freeze at the nauseating sight that awaits us. This room was originally several rooms before walls were torn down to make it one large cell. There are no windows. Beds line both sides. A single bathroom is lit at the far end, the door open. Other small lamps light up somewhere around forty trembling women huddled in groups, all with bellies.

In horror and loud enough for everyone to hear, Honey Badger says, "They're all pregnant!"

Scratch grabs his arm. "Shhhh."

Our faces are contorted in an attempt to restrain horror, confusion and shock as we realize this is a baby-making factory. My guess is it's probably for infertile women who want to adopt, and who will never know where their children really came from.

Struck at the sadness, abuse and loss these women have endured, we're all wondering the same thing, *how long has this been going on?*

"It's okay," Scratch announces to the women, holding up his hands. "We're here to help."

By his side I also reassure them, "It's over! It's all over."

Tonk and Honey Badger puts their guns in their belts again to hold their hands up, too.

"You're safe, ladies," Honey Badger says in as gentle a tone as he is capable of.

One of the women believes us, because her sobs twist immediately to those of deep relief. She crumbles to the ground and Tonk rushes forward to embrace her, kneeling by her side. She's about five, maybe six months to her due date and she can't be more than eighteen.

He looks at us, his face total agony. "Who would do this?"

Scratch mutters, "We have to call the police on this one."

Several women scream, "NO!" which shocks the fucking shit out of us.

In hurried cries of terror they beg us not to, some

speaking in English, others in Spanish. It's a big mess of female, terrified voices and weeping. We quickly realize they think the cops have been dirty all along. They think the police and government as a whole, knowingly let this happen.

"Fuck," Scratch rasps, overcome by the insidiousness of how deep this goes.

I raise my voice with patience and leadership. This is what I'm good at — calming people.

"Ladies! Ladies, listen to me for a minute. LADIES!" The room goes quiet and dozens of big, scared eyes lock on me. "Some of you speak English, so please, when I'm done, translate this for the others." I pause. "The police do NOT know you're here. They *are* your friends. They have *no idea* what you've been through and they *can* help you. They want to help, just like we do. You have been lied to and I'm very sorry for that. I am deeply, deeply sorry for what you've been through. My friends and I are here to set you free. We need to call the police, get you medical attention to make sure your babies are okay, and you will have many, many people working together to get you homes." As the glimmer of hope shines back from some of them, I pause, trying hard to keep my voice steady. I've never seen something as sick as this shit, and it's fucking killing me. "It's hard to believe. I can see you're scared and you have no reason to trust men. But I promise you we are different. You are about to discover *I'm* honest. *My friends* are honest. We are telling you the truth. See my face? This is *an honest man* looking at you. We are here to save you. This shit you've been through – it's over. It's done. Forever."

The room is dead silent. Tonk pets the young woman's dark hair before he rises up to join us so that we can stand in one powerful line together and show them we are not evil.

We mean what we say.

We will keep our word.

Scratch mutters, "We need to make sure none of those evil fucks gets away." He calls out to the women, "We're going to make sure the men who've hurt you are taken care of. Then we'll get you out of this hellhole. It's going to be okay."

The English speakers start translating, but of course trust is earned and this will be an uphill ride.

We head out.

"I wish we'd brought more Ciphers," Scratch says after the door is closed.

Honey Badger's mind is working and he grabs our V.P.'s arm. "There's not that many guys here. Ten, twelve? I don't know, but I bet they didn't need more because – and I fuckin' hate to say this – but this place looks like a well-oiled machine."

With disgust, Tonk growls, "Since they lied to the women about the police, I bet they never try to escape."

On a long exhale, Scratch asks Tonk, "You have the rope?"

He nods. "It's in my bags."

"Jesus, no wonder you never change your pants. You don't have any room in there," Honey Badger mutters.

"Hey, I'm prepared for shit like this," Tonk shoots back.

We all make quick strides back to find Fuse kicking one of the bodyguards in the gut.

"He was getting up. I got that one over there, too." Fuse points to a mess in the corner. He nods with amusement in his eyes. His nose is a dripping, bloody mess and his jacket is gonna need a sewing job.

"Good thing you got shot," I tell him, staring at the man he kicked. "Kept you out here keeping watch."

Soon we're cutting rope with pocketknives and tying up the fallen evil. I hear a noise and look up. To say the staircase is ornate would be a fuckin' understatement.

"Did we check upstairs?" Everyone shakes their heads. "Someone's up there. I'll go."

Honey Badger tightens the knot around the ankles of a thug and rises to come with.

Scratch warily looks upstairs and exhales through

his nose. He swipes a couple machine guns from where they fell, and hands them to Fuse and Tonk. "I'll protect the women and guard their door. Fuse, you make sure no one gets out the front. Tonk, check the other rooms on this floor. Jett, Honey, grab those rifles on your way."

Everyone breaks off. Honey Badger and I do as we're told and then stalk our way up the gaudy-ass staircase, but I'm sure whoever's up there heard us talking.

They know we're on our way. I feel calm. Ready to strike. I know Honey Badger feels the same. He's great under pressure. I feel sorry for the fuckers we're about to meet.

As we make our way down a long hallway, the second floor is quiet as a graveyard after a funeral. We carefully open doors to empty rooms decorated in the most expensive furniture money can buy.

At the far end one is cracked and waiting for us.

I've suddenly got a feeling in my gut I don't like.

Honey Badger looks at it, then back to me.

I nod.

Crouched, we approach and duck as a man jumps out and starts shooting. We meet his shots with our own and he falls in a grunting, jerking heap.

I kick the door open and we both freeze.

An elderly man is in a bed fit for a king. He's on

oxygen, watching us with wrinkly eyes that have an odd smile pulling at their edges. In front of the bed is Sunshine, tied up in a velvet red chair, her mouth covered with duct tape. Her beautiful eyes go wide at the sight of me.

Honey Badger shouts, "JETT!"

JETT

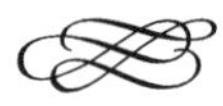

Ducking just in time, a bullet zips past my head. Honey Badger rushes the guy hiding behind the door. As I stride over to Sunshine another gunshot explodes through the room. I look over my shoulder to see if my friend is okay. He nods at me, his rotund body rising up as he grunts. The thug took the bullet. He's down.

"Search for more!" I growl as I reach her, setting down the machine gun by her feet. "You okay?"

She nods.

"They hurt you?"

She shakes her head.

"This is gonna hurt," I warn as I rip the duct tape off.

She gasps for air and handles the pain like a soldier.

"All clear," Honey Badger assures me, returning and staying by the door, just in case. "This is the last room upstairs." The old man watches us with rasping breaths echoing pathetically off the walls. The machine is making a pathetic sound, but I don't like the look in this guy's eyes. This guy is the big honcho. There's no doubt in my mind. On his nightstand are bottles of pills and...her 9mm.

"What are you doing here," she demands, voice hoarse from fear and bondage.

Untying the ropes on her wrists and ankles, I joke, "It was either this or rob a bank."

I assumed the old man couldn't talk.

I was wrong.

"Is this your boyfriend?" he rasps with the shittiest smirk. "Come to *save you*?"

She kicks off the rest of the bindings and stands to face him. "Fuck you." She grabs my machine gun and backs away, aiming at him.

My hands go up and I step toward her. "Whoa. Sunshine."

She aims the gun at me. "Get back to where you were!"

I'm no idiot. I do as I'm told. Honey Badger and I exchange a look as she points the gun at the old man again. It's a bizarre picture. A guy in his eighties – hell, maybe nineties – whose body has given out on him, shrouded in a four poster bed with black curtains, and a beautiful woman aiming a gun at his head.

"You didn't get what you want after all," she snarls.

"I did," he rasps with that evil smile. "You're in my bedroom."

Furious, she centers her aim. "You piece of shit, I hope you rot in hell." Her finger starts to press the trigger and I picture her in prison for the rest of her life.

"Don't do this."

"You don't know what he's done," she growls to me, determined, but scared. She's probably never killed anyone before. If that's true, it gives me enough of a chance to maybe talk her out of this. I'm gonna give it my best try.

"Sunshine...listen...I'm aware of the women downstairs. I know this guy is the boss and leader. But look at him. You won't be able to call this self-defense. You'll go to jail for murder. Or be on the run your whole fuckin' life."

She doesn't even look my way. He is the only thing she can see. "I've been on the run anyway! At least now he'll be gone. He'll be where he belongs. Do you know what he did?"

"I saw."

Staring at him with memories playing across her eyes, Sunshine whispers, as though she didn't hear me, "He preys on people. He spent his life making money off lonely women. Women who didn't have families, who didn't have anyone to help them. He sold them like cattle. For sex. And it didn't matter who wanted it. The evilest men in the world walked in, and he took their money and told them to do whatever they wanted. Like their lives meant nothing. All they wanted was a home and he twisted their dreams into nightmares." Tears start to fall down her cheeks as her steady hand begins to shake. "My mother was murdered by one of those animals. And he's lying there smiling at me!"

I look over. She's right.

The sick fuck is grinning.

I want to go punch the old bastard myself, now.

Honey Badger walks up and stops two feet behind me, silently wanting the same. But this is her fight.

I try one last time. "You willing to go to jail for life? We're calling the police. They'll take him away. You don't have to do this."

"Yes, I do," she whispers, bringing the gun up and closing one eye for aim.

The demon in the bed throws ice into my veins as he rasps something I never saw coming.

"So...you're gonna kill your own father?"

She doesn't even blink.

"Matias...I can't wait. Tell Lucifer you're home." Sunshine steadies the machine gun and fires. The old man's chest explodes. Then his face as she fires again.

I watch her trembling lips part as the gun falls from her hands. Relief laced with finality is all over her. She turns her head and gazes at me with a silent question. I can hear her asking as though she said aloud.

Is it over?

I nod and start to go to her. But a shot rings out. Her eyes lose their sad light and she crumples to the ground. I rush forward, darting a look behind to understand what just happened. The thug, the one we thought was dead, wasn't.

As Honey Badger runs to take him down, time slows. Everything is fuzzy as I scoop up the woman I held in my arms last night, and watch blood stream from the side of her head.

I am rocking her.

Shouting for an ambulance.

Whispering to her to hang on.

She's limp and heavy.

The blood won't stop.

"Stay with me."

JETT

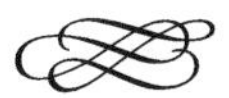

Scratch runs into the room and looks around. "What the fuck!!"

"GET AN AMBULANCE!" I yell.

He rushes to me, taking her in. "We did. Called the police, too. We're going to have to do a lot of explaining. And we're probably going to jail for this."

I barely hear him. I'm holding her, covered in her blood. "Stay with me, Sunshine. Fight!"

"I've got an idea!" Honey Badger cries out. "Scratch, come with me!"

They disappear. Time is frozen, and yet there they are again, carrying a guy in from outside. "Careful not to let his feet drop." To me, as if I care, Honey Badger says, "He's already dead."

They bring him over and lay him beside her, slump him like he was facing the bed. Scratch holds him up and leans way back. Honey Badger runs over to the unconscious guy by the door, the one who shot her.

"Jett, duck!"

I cover her with my body and bend out of the way.

He picks up the guy's gun, aims and fires at the dead thug. Scratch swears under his breath as the blood spatters on him and us. The now twice-dead body slumps to the side, his head a fuckin' unrecognizable mess. Scratch takes the gun Sunshine used and wipes her fingerprints off. He puts it in the dead guy's hand and makes sure the guy's fingerprints are on it in all the right places. Then he uses his shirt to wipe his own off.

Turning to me, Scratch sees my dazed expression.

I can't stop whispering to Sunshine.

I can't stop.

"Jett, focus! This is the deal."

My eyes slowly move to listen. Honey kneels in front of me. "This guy shot HIM." He points to Matias in the bed. "She went to *save* him. The old guy. She went to save him, you hear me?" I nod once. "And when she did, that guy shot this guy to save his boss, and accidentally hit her, too." He jabs a finger at the guy by the door, the fucker who caused my anguish. "You got it?"

"Stay with me, Sunshine," I whisper to her, nodding to my chosen brothers that I understand. At some point later I will thank them for clearing her name. That man fathered her. Then sold her mother as a whore. I can only imagine how that went down. Sunshine deserves peace, and respect for her bravery today.

She's got my respect.

"Hear those?" Scratch mumbles, as sirens get louder. "We ready for this?"

"Yeah," Honey Badger mutters, looking from me to the door.

I say nothing, but they know I'm good for it. We trust each other with our lives.

They go downstairs and I stay put. Again time tricks me. Suddenly EMTs are in the room telling me I have to let her go. I barely know this girl. I don't even know her fuckin' name. But I witnessed something in her. It began last night when she gave herself to me. It deepened tonight when I learned her story. I witnessed her enact a vengeance that she'd waited her whole life to do, and that kind of thing bonds you to a person.

I saw her soul tonight. Hell, I saw it last night, too. She took her wall down for me. How I earned that honor, I'll never know.

And now it's over.

"I'm going with you," I whisper, following them as they carry her out on a gurney.

Cops are everywhere. Searching. Listening.

The Ciphers are answering questions.

When two police officers try to stop me at the front door, my voice is firm. "I'll answer anything you want. But I'm not letting her out of my sight."

"How do we know you won't leave the hospital?"

"Do I look like I'm going anywhere she's not?"

They stare at me.

Fuse yells from behind his broken nose. "We're the good guys here! Let him go!"

"I'll go with him," a female cop says to the guy. "Cantor and I will make sure he stays put."

I head out. The EMTs have her in the ambulance and are about to close the door. One looks over his shoulder to see what the verdict is, if I'm coming or not. That's decent of him. I motion to the bike and he nods.

Climbing onto my baby, I flip the ignition. The familiar roar calms me. Centers me. Reminds me who I am. I'm Jett Fucking Cocker. I can handle this. And if these cops wanna put us in jail, they're going to have to fight me for the right. We help people, goddammit. They need men like us. Something my father doesn't want to believe, except when it serves him to use me to his own ends.

Sunshine...I thought I had problems with my old man. You win.

As we speed down the canyons of Los Angeles to Cedars Sinai Hospital, cars pull over for the ambulance and do double takes at the biker then the police car, whispering to each other, "What the hell happened there?"

JETT

A cup of coffee is thrust into my hands and I look over. "Take it," Honey Badger gruffly says. "You look like hell."

"If I see another cop again..."

He nods and sits on the beige, uncomfortable hospital chair on the other side of Sunshine's bed.

"Yeah," he mutters, staring at her bandaged head.

I take a sip as I gaze at her. It tastes like nothing to me. My senses are dead. Everything feels like how she looks – colorless and empty.

"What'd the doctor say?"

I inhale and shake my head. "I'm waiting to hear. They just wheeled her in."

Entering the room Fuse interjects, "Doctors are

just educated guessers, that's what my mom called them."

I look over to see him carrying his bloodied jacket, his shoulder gauzed. "They fix you up?"

He shrugs and rips the small piece of tape off his nose. "Fuck this thing. First time I've been to a real doctor since I joined the club eleven years ago. Felt weird. Didn't like it. But they did a cleaner job removing the bullet than you fuckers ever did."

Honey Badger adjusts in his chair to ask, "Well?"

Fuse leans against a wall and hooks his fingers in his blood-spattered jeans pockets. We're all covered. "After you guys finished answering all their fuckin' questions, they double fact-checked everything, asking the same things to us. Course all our stories are the same, because we're the fuckin' good guys here, but they sure didn't want to believe it, did they?"

We both shake our heads.

"Well, they're real curious about The Ciphers now. I have a feeling word might spread. In a good way. Hell, who knows how that'll pan out? Could put us up against other clubs. I don't know. Then Scratch and Tonk wanted to see what would happen to the girls, so they're at the precinct now. Said they'd call and find out where we are when they're done. I guess Tonk took a liking to one of the women, and he's real concerned over what happens to her after this. They don't have families. Most of them are totally alone."

Honey Badger and I look at each other as he tells me, "The one he consoled, probably, that's the one. Fuse was in the other room kicking ass."

"Right," I mutter, looking back at Sunshine. Gently I lift her hand and hold it, closing my eyes. I have a strong feeling she's gonna die on me. Never seen anyone this pale.

"Oh, here's somethin' interesting. That money she stole? The credit card thing?"

I look over at Fuse. "Yeah?"

"There was a van parked down from the palace of misery. It was stolen. Cops broke in right in front of us. Stacks of sealed up, brand new comforters."

"What the hell?" Honey Badger asks, frowning.

I look at Sunshine again. "Fuck. She thought she was gonna save those women. The blankets were for them."

Fuse's voice is low as he explains, "Scratch figured that out, too. He told the cops. Adds to her being there for noble reasons. Clears any doubt of..." He trails off.

"Good," I whisper, holding her hand to my forehead and closing my eyes.

Fuse and Honey go silent.

We stay like this.

From time to time I hear the slurping of coffee, but nothin' else.

After who knows how long, footsteps, the door opening, and Scratch's familiar voice, makes me turn my head. I feel stiff everywhere.

"Jett." He lays a heavy hand on my shoulder. "We got a hotel room. Go get cleaned up."

"I'm not leavin.'"

He wants to argue, but decides against it.

"Where's Tonk?" Fuse asks while Honey waits by the door.

"It's a fuckin' mess with those women. Social services and detectives all over the place. Some of them have distant relatives; some even had parents who didn't know where they were. Tonk's askin' about Carmen."

"That's her name?" Honey Badger asks.

"Yeah. She was clingin' to him for dear life until the cops made her let go. She's only eighteen."

"You know that for sure?"

"Yeah. There were records of the girls. He demanded to know if she was underage on top of everything. Some of them were younger than eighteen when they got impregnated."

"Fuckin' animals," Honey Badger growls.

"You said it. Carmen turns nineteen soon, so she wasn't a minor. Tonk looked like he was gonna kill someone if she had been. He's taken a real liking to the girl."

The door opens again and a man in a lab coat enters.

I stand up for answers. "Is she gonna make it?"

He glances around the room. We're a sight, the four Ciphers. Only our hands are washed clean. Fuse looks like a truck hit him. After him, I'm the worst and it's mostly her blood.

The doctor pauses to gather his cool and turns wary eyes to me. "Look, it's against our protocol to give you information when you're not family." He raises his hand as I begin to speak. "BUT I am making an exception. I heard about what happened. I think you guys deserve to know, after what you all did." He glances around our somber faces. "She's in a coma. The bullet skimmed the side of her skull. It didn't hit her brain tissue, but there was internal bleeding. As a result, she's in a coma and we don't know any more than that."

Grasping for straws, I ask, "She's not going to die?"

"I didn't say that. Not everyone makes it out of a coma. I'm sorry, but they are unpredictable. The body has gone to sleep to heal from the trauma, but she might not...I'm sorry."

The Ciphers are all staring at me with stone faces. I blink back to her and rasp, "How long are comas? For how long? I mean, is there a normal amount of time?"

"People have come out in days, weeks, months... sometimes years. There's still much we don't know about them."

"There's still much you don't know about a lot of shit," Fuse grumbles.

The doctor pauses and glances over. He sighs. "True. But we will do the best we can to save her life. This is one of the best hospitals in the country."

"Can she hear me?"

"People have reported hearing things when they were unconscious, yes. Not everyone, but I think it's worth doing, just in case. It certainly can't hurt." He pauses, walking to thumb through her folder. "I thought you might want to know that we have to call her Jane Doe."

My head whips to him and his steady gaze falters.

"What the fuck," I growl.

"I'm sorry, Mr. Cocker, but the police don't have a record of her. There are no fingerprints in their system. She had no I.D. in her backpack or on her person." He sees the storm brewing in me, and cautiously adds, "And they said you didn't know her name."

"Jesus," Scratch mutters.

I grab the folder from him, looming over the guy. "Give me that pen." Hesitating, he hands it to me. I cross out the fucking *Jane Doe* and scrawl above it, *Sunshine.*

"There. Call her that until she wakes the fuck up."

Honey Badger looks over the doc's shoulder and smiles proudly as the guy reads it, too. After a long beat, he does the decent thing. "I'll have them change it in the system. We'll print out a new one."

Turning to her, I take a seat, pick up her hand and firmly tell the room, "Go."

One after the other, they file out.

Scratch is the last one, and he walks over to pat my shoulder. "Call."

I nod and wait until the door closes behind him.

"Sunshine, if you can hear me, you did good back there tonight. You did it. It's over." A lump tightens in my throat. "If you have to go now, I understand. You deserve to have whatever you want, but...I want you to stay. *I want you to stay.*" Holding her clammy hand to my forehead, I close my eyes.

JETT

For the next few days, I eat here in the room, watching her face and listening to the machine that's breathing for her. The nurses brought me in a cot to sleep on. Every two hours when they come in, and it's the same thing — they apologize for waking me and I tell them I wasn't sleeping.

My brothers check on me during this time. Scratch tells me the story hit the Los Angeles Times: Who Are Your Neighbors Really?

The journalist left out the part about the Ciphers.

Fine by us.

We don't want publicity.

Let the cops take the win. They sure fucking need one.

On day three, I hear the door open and at the

sound of many heavy boots, I glance over to see all four Ciphers have come.

I blink at their determined expressions.

Fuse, Honey Badger and Tonk all cross their arms, and I notice their jackets are clean now. Fuse's shoulder has the hole in it. He plans to leave it that way.

Scratch stands in front of them. "Time for a fuckin' shower and some real sleep."

"No." I turn back to her.

A great force pulls me up from the chair and I fight off Tonk and Scratch.

"FUCKIN' PUT ME DOWN!" Despite my exhaustion, I break my right arm free and punch Honey Badger as he moves in from the front to help.

He punches me in the gut and I double over. "JETT, GO TAKE A MOTHERFUCKIN' SHOWER."

Panting with Tonk and Scratch holding onto my arms, I glare at them. "What are you, my mothers?"

Fuse levels on me, leaning in. "You smell like shit. If she can smell, you aren't doin' her any favors by bein' here like this."

I hear the logic. But I don't like it. Snarling, I tell them, "Let me go."

"You gonna be a good boy?" Scratch asks.

I cut my eyes to him and see the smile in his.

"Fuck you. Fine." Releasing me, they throw me my jacket. "Who's stayin' with her?"

"I will," Tonk says. His eyes say I can trust him.

"Fine." To the room, I growl, "Give me a minute alone with her." They file out. Fuckin' assholes.

I've been obsessed. Somewhere deep inside I know it, but the thought of leaving her alone is fuckin' killing me.

But they're right. I'm a mess. I'm no good to her like this. "Sunshine," I say as I walk to her side and feel a lump forming in my damn throat. "Remember how I said it was okay to leave? Well, not yet. If you fuckin' clock out while I'm gone, I will hunt you down in heaven and make you pay for that shit." I lean over with tears in my eyes. "I mean it. Don't leave yet. I'll be back. Tonk's gonna watch over you. Don't you fuckin' leave." Kissing her cheek, I hold there. It takes every ounce of willpower I have to walk away.

LUNA

It feels like I've drunk five liters of Jack Daniels. I open my eyes, but nothing is in focus. There is a distant beep, but other than that, silence.

Is this a dream?

Shapes come into focus. A beige rectangle. A black square high above that. A huge white blob to my left.

Am I paralyzed?

Wiggling my toes takes everything I've got, but I do feel them moving.

It's like this fog doesn't want to leave.

I'm confused. Lost. Bone-weary.

My hand is warm. So are my thighs. They feel heavy as if someone is holding them down.

Am I chained up?

Did Matias's men drug me?

I have to stay quiet in case they are listening.

If they think they've won, they're wrong.

I will get out of here.

I will never give up.

Something is in my nose. It hurts. The white blur to my left becomes a curtain. I look down and see a bearded man sleeping on my legs. My hand is warm because his is. Our fingers are entwined. He looks familiar.

He looks like...

Oh...

I remember now.

I snuck into the mansion thinking I was being so sly. But they were watching me, acting like they didn't see me coming. They tied me up. He sneered and wondered aloud what he should do to me. His bodyguards had waited, enjoying it.

Then the explosion of action. "Someone's here!"

Matias rasped from his bed, "Go get whoever the fuck it is!"

I glared at him with the hate of all the women he'd hurt, glad to see him sick and frail with cancer. If I died that night at least I knew he'd follow soon after.

But that wasn't enough.

One of those men was his son. I found that out when I was being gagged. He was due to inherit the business and perpetuate what they'd done. And then another man would take over. And another. And it would never end.

They had to die, but I didn't know how. I had machine guns pointed at my head and no way to break free of the bindings, to grab them.

And then Jett appeared, with his Tasmanian Devil friend. He didn't want me to do it. But then he found out the truth.

I pulled the trigger over and over. Turned and looked into his eyes and saw understanding and respect.

And it was done.

But where am I now? I don't understand. Staring at him asleep on my legs, I try to speak but my mouth is dry. My jaw feels stiff.

Barely able to move my fingers, I squeeze his hand. Like a gun went off in the room, Jett sits upright and looks around. Then at me. His beautiful eyes go wide, staring at me with shock.

He jerks forward in his chair, clasping my hand to his hard chest as he reaches to touch my face. "Sunshine?"

I nod my head just a little; it's all I can do.

A grin grows on his face and he shouts, "NURSE! NURSE!!!" His eyes go dark and he asks me, "Do you know who I am?"

Parting my lips, I painfully rasp, "Jett."

He whoops and rises up, fist-pumping the air like an idiot.

"Water," I whisper.

While still gripping my hand to his body, he cranes back to grab one from a rickety tray-table, and brings it to my lips. Lifting my other hand takes effort, but I do succeed in taking the small glass and nodding to him that I've got it.

"Holy shit, look at you!" he whispers like I just performed a miracle just by holding this cup.

"NURSE!!! SHE'S AWAKE!" he shouts at the door.

Swallowing is painful. I've never felt this way before. "Where are we?" I croak. "What happened?"

Those grey eyes of his cloud over as the smile disappears.

"Oh, Sunshine baby, you've been in a coma. You've been out for a long time."

Fear pulls at me and all I can do is raise my eyebrows with the question I'm too frightened to ask.

Low and cautious, he tells me, "It's been three months. Seven days."

The door explodes with three nurses, and they all tell Jett to stand back. He doesn't fight them, which surprises me. He and I are staring at each other as the nurses pull at cords attached to my body, fiddle with what I now realize is oxygen tubes in my nose. Doctors come in next. There is a lot of action. I'm questioned about whether or not I know who I am. I nod.

Then they ask me my name.

It's Jett's face I'm looking at when I answer, "Luna."

His eyes fill with a man's kind of emotion, the kind that's distant and full and confusing to him.

"What's your last name?" the doctor asks.

Still on Jett, I whisper, "I don't have one." His lips tighten as he pushes off the wall.

"Alright, let her rest."

The doctors don't listen to him. He stands by as they inform him there are many things they need to check due to the severity of my head trauma. I have to wiggle toes and fingers for them. I have to recite dates. And finally when they're satisfied, they tell us both I'll have to stay to be supervised until they know it's safe. As they file out, one of the nurse's looks over her shoulder at Jett with a small smile. He doesn't notice.

He pulls the chair back to my bed from where they moved it, and sits down, grabbing my hand immediately. "How you doin'?"

"Not used to the attention," I whisper. He hands me more water and I drink it on my own. He takes it and sets it down and I notice his hand is shaking.

"Luna," he murmurs to himself before he meets my eyes. "That's the moon in Spanish?"

"Yeah."

"It's the opposite of Sunshine," he says with an attempt at a smile. Despite the effort, I can tell he's shaken.

I get it. I don't know what to do with him either.

"You called me that as a joke," I whisper. It's all I can do. My voice hasn't been used in months and my throat feels terrible.

"At first." He pauses. "Must be weird losin' all that time." I nod. "You want to know what happened?"

"Yes."

The story unravels as he explains what he knows, from beginning to now. He's a man, so the details are blunt and brief. When he tells me the women were pregnant, I gasp. His handsome face registers surprise. "You didn't know that?"

"No."

"You used to live there, didn't you?"

Shaking my head a little, I rasp, "Different house. They were prostitutes. They all took the pill."

I used to watch them take it every day, given to them like clockwork at eight o'clock every morning, like the drugs they give inmates in an insane asylum.

"What is that, Mommy?"

"It's to make sure we stay in business, Luna."

I only learned what that meant later on, when I was adult enough to understand.

"Why pregnant?"

Jett leans back in the chair. "You can make a lot more money selling babies. A lot of infertile women in the world dying to be mothers."

Horror dives into my bloodstream. I remember the disappearing babies, the ones where the pill either didn't work, or the women didn't swallow. It must have given *him* the idea.

Jett rises from the chair and takes me into his arms. "Shhhh...it's over."

"Oh my God," I stutter into the soft, black t-shirt. "He's...so...evil!"

"He's *dead,* Sunshine. He's dead, baby. It's over. You did it." We stay like this until the sobs stop. Jett kisses my hair and looks in my eyes. "They're safe now. A lot of them are reunited with family. Donations came in from all over. Some women got homes together." I nod, sniffling. He reaches for a tiny hospital box of tissues and hands me one, shaking his head and muttering, "It's a lot of fuckin' therapy but they're gonna be okay now."

He gets up and walks to the door to make sure it's closed. When he returns, I know something big is coming. In a low volume he tells me how his friends fixed it so I look like I was saving Matias.

Anger flashes into me. "I would never save him!"

"No no no!" Jett holds his hands up to stop me.

"Don't get excited. Think about where you'd be right now if we didn't. With all those girls and the condition they were in? We had to call the police. We NEVER call the police. Understand? We had to make you the hero. Which you fuckin' are!" He lowers his voice to somberly add, "But the law wouldn't see it that way."

I'm so upset. I know he's right, but it still makes me furious for anyone to believe I'd come to that bastard's aid.

"I'd rather be in jail."

Jett goes for my hand but I tug it back. "Luna, *you* know the truth. That's all that should matter. I stopped caring about what other people thought of me a long time ago."

Meeting his eyes, I stare at him. He's right.

I'm too stubborn to tell him that.

"You just called me Luna," I whisper, glancing away.

JETT

They removed the bandages when the wounds healed, two weeks and two days after her surgery. Over the past few months I've left the room only so they could wash her hair and clean her up. The side of her head is shaved, and growing back nicely over a scar. She looks like she got that cool haircut on purpose—half-shaved, the other long and wavy.

They brought in a better bed for me when they figured out I planned to stay.

I've been here every day and night.

When a male, well-built physical therapist arrived, he told me he was there to move her limbs around so that her circulation stayed healthy and she didn't get bedsores. I put that brakes on that. "Show me how to do it, then take a hike."

Pretty sure I've watched every episode of Law and Order, which is a fuckin' lot. Castle and CSI, too. I'm pissed they cancelled Castle without an official season finale. That's bullshit right there. It's like closing up a book series without writing about the final wolf. What the fuck? Must have had a good reason...but I hate it just the same.

The Ciphers left a few days after the cops gave us leave to. All except Tonk.

He's been seeing Carmen and taking it really slow since she's of course pretty messed up. Eager to heal, though. She's a brave girl deep down, no matter how fragile she appears. They didn't get any sunlight in that place, so he's been taking her to parks and to the beach almost every day.

Since she never thought she'd escape that place, she views everything on the outside with wonder and a little fear, except him.

Him she looks at like a god.

He's upside down in love with her. I respect the hell out of how he's treatin' that girl.

As I return from asking the nurse when she can eat, Luna whispers "You don't have to stay."

"Yeah, right," I mutter.

This one's not like Carmen at all.

This one fights me at every turn.

And I don't seem to give a shit. She woke up late last night. So this is officially day one of the battle.

I'm all in.

Grabbing a bag from the dresser, I pull out toothpaste and a toothbrush that's still in the package. Bought these for when this miracle would happen. Gave me hope to have them ready.

She watches me tear it open and walk to fill one of those vomit dishes they have handy, with fresh water from the sink. It's never been used — cleaner than my own fingers.

The tray table is an awkward sonofabitch so I have to work not to splash.

I swear at it under my breath.

"What are you doing?" she asks.

"Your breath stinks."

She smiles in surprise. "Jesus," she mutters.

I chuckle because I could care less about her fuckin' ass-breath, which really is terrible. I only said that and am doing this to break the iceberg she's erected now that she realizes she can't run.

The girl likes it straight and honest. Some women would call it rough, but they're not made of iron like this one.

I can give her what she needs. I can talk her language.

Cocking an eyebrow, I ask, "You want me to do it for you like a little baby?"

With a weak arm, she grabs the toothbrush after I squeeze blue goo on it. "Fuck you."

"Let's get your strength back and we'll talk about fuckin' again."

Her deep brown eyes dance with amusement and she brushes her teeth slowly, stopping to say, "It tastes strong."

"Bet my cum tastes better."

She huffs a laugh and shakes her head like I'm an asshole, spitting out some foam and continuing the difficult journey.

I stop watching, pick up my Ciphers jacket and ask, "You gotta use the bathroom?" She reluctantly nods. "I'll get a nurse."

Outside my heart is pounding. I feel like that smile and half-laugh she gave up was a win on my part. One I've waited a long fuckin' time for. At the nurse's station I have their full attention. Karen watches me as she always does. She'd love me to take her somewhere private. Not subtle, this one. I couldn't care less.

"You must be so happy, Jett!" Ellen gushes.

"Yeah. When can she eat real food?"

Diego walks up and hears this. "We'll bring her soft food first and see how she handles it."

"Thanks."

Nice guy, but I still can't believe a man who's not gay wants to be a nurse. "Congratulations!" he says.

"I didn't do anything," I call back as I walk off, pulling my phone from my jacket pocket.

Dialing, I wait for Tonk to answer, "Hey."

"Guess what."

After a beat, he goes, "No way."

"She's up."

"Holy fuck! What's she like?"

"A pain in the ass."

He chuckles. "So...she's healthy then."

"If you can call it that," I say with a big smile.

LUNA

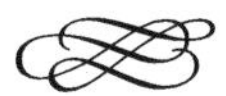

"We'll be back in a couple hours to check on you again," the young, attractive nurse tells me.

"Okay."

She leaves and glances over to Jett with longing. "Isn't his beard handsome?" she asks me while *staring* at him. I'm sure he has admirers wherever he goes, but still, she has some fucking nerve doing this in front of me.

She disappears.

I glance over to see his reaction...and discover him climbing in the small, extra bed.

"Don't say it," Jett warns with a suspicious look. Somehow I know he's not talking about the nurse. He knows my mind has switched gears now that I see he's planning on sleeping here tonight.

"What the hell are you doing?"

He's got his pillow on the foot side of the bed so he can see me. I saw the bed, earlier. I just haven't been able to bring myself to ask the question: *Have you been here every night?*

It's too big.

But now there's no avoiding it with him untying his boots. "I'm goin' to sleep. It's been a busy day. You came back to life. I had to force you to eat carrot soup. You nearly spit out the applesauce. You didn't know your breath stank. Phew. I'm beat!"

Fighting back a smile, I hoarsely persevere. "You're not sleeping here!"

"Well, that'd be a change." He leans to the floor, grabs a wandering pillow from it and shoves it under the one he has. I watch his muscles undulate during the reach and his biceps contract as he rests his hands under his head, propping up. "There, now I can see you better," he smirks.

I can tell he's waiting for a reaction, so I take another route and give him none. "Goodnight then."

He blinks at me, knowing that was hard for me to do. "Night, Sunshine."

The nickname mushes my heart a little and I close my eyes and pull the blanket up. There's a small light on in the bathroom. He said he wanted it left on in case I had to go. You'd think this guy had kids or something.

Wait...does he?

I have no idea.

I remember very well what he looks like naked. The image is hard to shove away as I look at him, lying there peacefully, eyes are closed and the blanket half off his gorgeous body. He's sleeping in his jeans and t-shirt, socks stuffed in his boots to the side. Belt next to them.

"Jett?"

"Hmmm?"

"Do you have kids?"

After a long pause, he says, "Not yet."

Okay, I don't like how relieved I am to hear that.

"Why are you so good at taking care of people then?"

He opens his eyes and looks at me. In the dim light I watch his face soften as he tells me, "I have a good mother. And younger brothers who got into a lot of trouble growing up."

"How many brothers?"

"Five. Four younger. One older. And he never needed anyone taking care of him."

"You say that with pride."

"Jaxson's a good man. Keeps to himself. Loyal as fuck."

"Who else?"

"Justin and Jason are right below me. Twins. Different though. Justin's in politics and has the personality for it." Off my look, he corrects me. "He's a charmer, not a liar." I smile, and he continues, "Jason's a hopeless romantic. Produces crap music I can't listen to. You're free to mock that all you want. I do," he chuckles to himself, staring at the ceiling. "Then there's Jake. He's in construction. Hell of a work ethic. I guess we all have that. Jake's got the coloring of our mom — olive skin, brown eyes. Jeremy, too. He's the youngest. He's in Pakistan right now. Marines. Fuckin' kid's gonna be a bigger badass than I am. I'll have to punch him out. Make sure he knows his older brother is still in charge." He grins at me and looks so handsome that it's scaring me. "This tat?" He points to his pectoral muscle through his shirt. "We all have one."

I look down and start massaging my palm with my thumb to help my circulation, just as Jett taught me to do an hour ago. It was weird listening to him explain how I need to bend my knees often, and stretch out my ankles, too.

Here's that question again.

Have you been here every night? Have you been bending my legs for me when I couldn't?

Instead I whisper, "Wow. That's a big family."

He rolls onto his side and props himself up with a strong elbow. "Sunshine?"

From his voice I know he's about to say something that's going to be hard to hear, so I keep my eyes averted. "Hmmm?"

"I remember what you told me that night, about your mom. I'm real sorry 'bout that."

I nod and wait for more. When he remains quiet, I glance over. His eyes are heartbreaking because they're so fucking patient.

"I'm over it," I shrug, lying.

"No, you're not. You're probably never gonna be."

"No I probably won't." I whisper. I don't know why I confess this but it's out of my mouth before I realize I'm opening up to him. "I've never told anyone."

"About how she died?"

"About...any of it."

He nods and lies back down. Probably to avoid scaring me off. He does that a lot, leaves or looks away just when I'm about to get freaked. It just feels like he gets it. Like he knows me better than I do.

His eyes are closed and his arms are above his head again, resting on both hands. One knee is bent and I glance over to see he's wiggling his toes on the straight leg. The room is quiet for a long time while I drink him in and imagine him sleeping there, while I had no idea.

Was he really worried about *me*?

Is he here out of obligation?

Is it just because his friends are still in L.A.?

"Your friends don't mind you not staying in the motel?" I quietly ask.

After a beat of silence, he licks his lips. "They took off."

Shocked, I can't help but blurt out, "WHAT?"

He glances to me. That's the loudest I've said anything all day. I kinda shocked him.

"You stayed here on purpose?!"

He gets up and goes to stand by the door. He's about to leave. I've seen him do it about ten times since I woke up this morning. But he stops and holds onto the wall, his back tense and his legs staggered in decision. From that stance, where I can't see his face, he rumbles, "I have been here every night and every day."

My breath hitches.

Time slows way down.

I can hear my heart beating in my ears.

Jett strides back to me and cups my face with warm, large hands. "Sunshine, something happened to me when you came into my life. I need you. And you need me, too. I'm staying here until you get better and then I want you to come with me."

Tears jump to my eyes. "Where?"

"Everywhere."

He searches my eyes to gauge how I feel, then

leans down and kisses me softly, holding my face like I might break if he's not careful. My body responds. I can't help but return the kiss. But as the feelings overwhelm me, I push him away. "Stop. Please."

He backs off, hands in the air like I'm holding a gun on him. "Sorry. You need rest. I shouldn't have done that. I'm sorry. You just woke up..." he turns away and runs his hands through his hair, but not before I catch sight of the tent in his faded blue jeans. "...today after three fuckin' months and...I've waited so long." He turns to look at me and there is real pain in him. "I thought you were gonna die. I thought...you were gonna fuckin' die on me."

I don't know what to say, so I don't try.

He goes back to his sorry excuse for a bed — not nearly big enough for a man of his size — and lies down, pulling the blanket over his body and glancing to his own erection. Licking his lips for patience and because his feelings have been stirred up in a lot of ways, he leans back and stares at the ceiling, fighting to get ahold of himself.

And I'm watching all of it.

"It's so *much,* Jett."

"I know," he mutters.

"In my mind, we just met."

He exhales and whispers, "Yeah, I guess it would feel like that to you."

During the awkward silence that follows, he reaches under the blankets and adjusts himself, swearing under his breath.

The kisses and knowing what he's done for me, has stirred my body, too. But I'm too weak to do anything. The urge to touch this man is strong. I've never had a reaction to anyone like this. He's different.

But I'm not.

I'm me.

Still...I owe him. He'd never say that, but I do.

"Jett, would you do something for me?"

"Anything."

"Well, it's kind of...for you."

He glances over. "I don't need anything."

A small smile tugs at my mouth as I purposefully scan his blanket, hovering over the place where his erection is, and then meet his eyes again.

"Yes, you do."

He blinks. "What do you want me to do?" he asks carefully, and I can hear the curiosity in his voice. "Why am I gettin' the feeling you're gonna suggest sex? Because as much as I fuckin' want to, there's no way I'm risking' it."

"But you could take care of yourself." He stares at me. I lower to a whisper, the idea turning me on. "Jett, stroke yourself in front of me. I want to watch you make yourself feel good."

He sits up and leans on one arm, the muscles flexed under his weight. "You serious?"

"Mmmhmm."

Jett glances to the door and rises up, walking to the curtain. He pauses and looks at me, then pulls it shut.

There's a little bit of pain in his eyes as he walks to the side of my bed, like he's needed this. I lay my hand on his hip, slipping my fingers under his shirt and pressing them into his skin.

"You really wanna watch me stroke it for you?"

"Never done that before."

His eyes darken. "How many men have you been with?"

"You want me to ask you how many *women* you've been with?" I shoot back with a challenging smile.

But he isn't smiling at all. "How many?"

"Seriously?"

"Yep."

Sighing, I confess, "Very few, if you must know. Three." At his surprise, I hold his eyes. "Men and I have a history, Jett. No, don't feel bad. You didn't bring anything up. I'm just answering your ill-timed question."

"Just three before me."

"Including you."

He pauses and I can't read his expression. In a low rasp he asks the thing that was bugging him. "Did you love them?" He covers my hand with his, pressing it into his body. I glance to his white knuckles and tell him the truth.

"I've never been in love." Meeting his eyes, I ask, "You?"

Slowly unzipping his pants, he says with meaning, "Just once." Before I have a chance to register that, his enormous cock comes into view, almost full. It twitches up to meet his hand as he reaches for it.

He leans down, brings my hand to his lips and kisses my fingertips, then puts my hand where it was on his hip. "You strong enough to hold me there?"

I nod, my senses tingling. I was thinking I was doing this for him, but now that it's begun and I see him stepping out of those jeans all the way, and tug off that shirt, too, I've gotta admit...I need this, too.

This is life.

Feeling this awake when you're with someone.

Wanting to touch them.

Wanting them as close as you can get them.

He palms himself and groans as he begins to stroke that shaft. My eyes blaze a trail up to his face, over his abs and his chest rippling with halting breaths. Our eyes lock and his eyelids lower slightly as his lips fall open. "Fuck, I want to be inside you."

"Tell me what you'd do."

He groans and closes his eyes a brief second. "I'll

tell you what I WILL do," he grates through gritted teeth, gazing at me sensually. "The second we're outta here I'm gonna eat that sweet cunt until you scream again."

I dig my fingers into his hip.

"I'm going to shove my tongue in and taste that pussy all night long, baby. I'm gonna suck on your clit until you're quiverin' and then I'm gonna fuck you for days."

A moan escapes my lips and I lower my eyes to watch his hand speed up, sure and steady. The crimson tip appears and expands with every urgent stroke.

"I want to taste it," I whisper, my tongue on my teeth.

"No, baby. Not yet." He grabs my hand and laces our fingers together, stepping a little closer. The veins in his hips swell as he lets his body move with the beating. "I'm gonna prop you on this cock and watch you ride me like you did on that motel floor."

With my free hand I touch my breast through my gown and meet his eyes. He starts breathing more heavily. "Fuck, I love it when you do that, Sunshine. You know what else I'm gonna do to you?"

"What?"

"Lick your tits until you cum."

"That wouldn't make me cum," I smile.

"You wanna bet?" he smirks. A low groan escapes

him. "There will come a point when I'm doing it for so long that you let go and that's when I'll have you." His hand is moving faster now. Panting, he releases my fingers and rakes a hand through his hair. The underside of his bicep is paler than the top. Never sees the sun. His chest is stretched in this posture and he looks so delicious. I can't wait to see him explode. I grab onto his hip and dig my fingers in. He groans, pumping roughly.

I whisper, eager for it, "Cum for me, baby. I looooove watching this. You look incredible."

He groans and grits his teeth. I see his balls tightening so I reach down and gently cup them. He yells out really loudly and in another second hot semen shoots all over my arm. He locks eyes with me and firmly strokes that gorgeous shaft until every ounce is released.

The door opens as a female voice asks, "Everything okay?"

"WE'RE FUCKING!" he shouts. "CLOSE THE DOOR!"

"Oh my God," the nurse whispers from the other side of the curtain.

The door clicks back into place.

We burst out laughing. "I'll get a towel."

JETT

"Hey hey hey!" Tonk calls in, announcing his arrival from outside the hospital room before I even open my eyes.

With the recent turn of events I'm ecstatic to see him. Finally have good news after all these months.

My friends have been worried.

I get it.

They respect this, but I know most of 'em are wonderin' when I was gonna give up. Never once occurred to me to throw in the towel.

The Ciphers have done missions without me since they left L.A., but I told them I'd be back – I just didn't know when. I had faith. It wasn't easy watching the days pass and not knowing what would happen.

But it sure was worth it.

Glancing over to make sure she's awake, I receive a small, closed-mouth smile. Her color is better this morning. There's an orange juice on her little table. Must have slept through the last rounds of vitals checking.

I greet him with my morning voice, deep but happy. "Hey, Tonk! It's cool. Come on in."

Luna half-waves at him as he enters, looking like she feels a little like a creature in a zoo.

His eyes gleam at the sight of her. "Wow. Okay if Carmen comes in?" he asks, looking between me and Luna.

She doesn't know about Carmen.

I haven't had the chance to tell her and I'm not sure how she'll take it.

But I'm not making the girl sit outside in the corridor.

"Yeah, 'course. Bring her in. Just give us a minute."

"Sure. I'll get you some coffee from the cafeteria."

Throwing the blanket off me as my friend heads out, I walk the couple steps to Luna's bed. "She's one of Matias's girls, Sunshine." Her face contorts with surprise and confusion. In a hushed voice, I reassure her, "He's in love with the girl. Gonna take care of her *and* the baby."

"What?"

"Yeah. I'm gonna brush my teeth. You want help?"

With her mind now on Carmen, she mutters, "Just give me the thing full of water. I'll do the rest."

"You got it."

In no time Carmen — now nineteen and ready to pop — gets guided in to meet the woman who saved her, for the first time.

We were in it together, after all, in a weird roundabout way. It wasn't my idea for Tonk to tell Carmen that Luna's a hero, but he did it anyway because — the way he explained it to me — she did take out the bastard behind the whole cold-blooded enterprise. Permanently.

Carmen smiles with admiration and whispers a gentle, "Hello," then glances to me with a small nod. "Hello, Jett."

Luna's dark eyes are misty as she takes the girl in, huge stomach and all. She's clutching her hospital blanket, and the room is tense as we all wait for her to say something. She's just staring at Carmen, which is making the pregnant girl self-conscious. Tonk takes her hand protectively, but remains quiet. This is a dicey situation crackling with emotion. Tonk is aware of Luna's history, to the extent of what we know, which isn't much but enough.

Luna starts getting out of the bed, but stops and whispers, "Dizzy." She meets Carmen's eyes again, and holds out her hand. "Can you come here?"

Tonk releases her as he exchanges a look with me. I nod that I understand this is tense.

Carmen walks to the bed and nervously smiles. Sunshine offers her an open palm and the young, pregnant girl lays her hand on it. A tear slides down Sunshine's cheeks and she croaks, "I'm so sorry."

Carmen starts to cry. Luna rises up on her knees and encircles Carmen in a hug. The two women close their eyes and hold each other. Tonk and I drop our gazes to the floor to give them respectful privacy.

"Thank you for saving my life," Carmen whispers.

Luna pulls away, shaking her head. "It was them. It wasn't me."

Tonk's voice is hoarse now, too, but he's not having it. "No! It was all of us."

Carmen buries herself into his side as he goes to her, her belly pressed against his.

"You hear from Honey Badger?" he asks me, trying to change the subject for his own sanity. He really wishes he was the one who killed Matias. He's told me many times.

I get it.

I kinda wish I'd done it, too.

"Nah. What's up?" I cross my arms with my feet spread wide.

"Mission accomplished. He said it was a piece of

chocolate cake with gooey frosting after what we did here."

Smiling at the description, I say, "No doubt."

"Well," He smiles at Luna. "Carmen's due soon, so we were thinking of headin' home, but I'm glad we saw you alright before we left."

Tonk's manner has changed dramatically since Carmen has come into his life. He still looks like a huge badass, but his heart is on his sleeve now. There's a soft light in his eyes, and it shines like crazy when he looks at her like he's doing now.

My eyebrows knit as I think about what he's said. "Huh. Hadn't thought of the next move. Been busy."

I don't have to look to know Luna's watching me. I can feel her staring, wondering what I'm gonna do now.

Massaging Carmen's back with the hand that's holding her to him, Tonk explains, "I want the baby to be born there. Los Angeles isn't our home."

I mutter, under my breath, "Right. I guess I'll meet you there later on."

"Well, I was thinkin,' Jett, that she can't ride the back of my bike like this. And it's too late for flyin' — she can't go on airplanes at nine months, so...what about the train? Amtrak?"

"By herself?" I ask with a deep frown. "I don't like it."

Tonk's eyes drift to Luna and I realize what he's trying to get at. I look over to see her reaction. She's smart enough that she's caught on, too, that Tonk wants her to watch over Carmen for the trip, while we ride our motorcycles. The hopeful look on his face gives him away.

Fuck, I wish he would've brought this up with me, first. Springing it on her like this isn't a good idea. "Sunshine's just woke up, man."

"I know..."

"They haven't even set her free, yet."

"Yeah." He looks at Carmen. "Guess I'm gettin' anxious. Any day now."

"Two more weeks," I tell him.

"Anything can happen, man. I want the guys around. And Melodi and Hannah."

"Melodi's fuckin' nuts," I mutter, thinking of Fuse's crazy woman.

"She's good with kids, though. Just has a jealous streak, that's all."

With amusement I raise my eyebrows at him, remembering well his speech about how jealous bitches bring men down and that Fuse should leave his. But motivation changes opinions. And Melodi is a good mother. She's even better than Hannah whose got three runnin' around from Scythe. Since he's on the road the most of any of us, Melodi cares for Hannah's kids thanks to her depression from missing her man. It's a vicious circle, but we all take care of each other.

"True," I mutter, shaking my head at how twisted life is.

A nurse enters with the machine to check Luna's vitals. Behind her is that physical therapist I don't want near her. I straighten up and eyeball him. Tonk notices and glances over as the tight-shirted fuckhead nods to us, then smiles at Luna.

"Well, look at you!"

She frowns at him and glances to me. "Who the hell is this?" she asks me as the nurse wraps the blood pressure Velcro on.

Relief relaxes me into a low laugh. She doesn't find the dude attractive. Good. "He's gonna help you get stronger, baby."

She sneers from me to him. Perplexed by this reaction, he looks around with a lot less confidence than he walked in with. Tonk's trying not to laugh.

"Sunshine likes her men dirty," I tell the poor guy.

Luna laughs and tries to get serious as quickly as she can. "Sorry. What do you need me to do?"

As soon as the nurse finishes up, he guides Luna out of the bed and tells her, "It's normal to feel dizzy." Holding her up, he walks her around the small room until she finally pulls away.

"I think I've got it."

Tonk and I exchange a look, but Carmen is just watching Luna like she's the most interesting woman in the world. There's an invisible pedestal erecting under her bare feet with every passing second.

Holding onto the wall, Luna walks around and breathes deeply in and out. The hospital therapist watches her and walks with her, but doesn't dare make a move to help.

She glances to me out of the corner of her beautiful eyes, and smiles. "I'm gonna be fine."

I'm feeling more pride than I ever have for anything or anyone, ever.

"*Yeah* you are," I tell her. "You're gonna be better than fine, baby."

LUNA

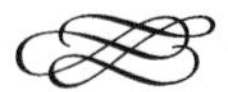

I groan, "Mmm..." as I take another bite of the Fatburger Jett brought me. "This is amazing."

"Best in town," he grins, chomping on one of his own. "And best name for a burger place, ever."

We eat in silence for a while.

When a nurse knocks on the door, he calls to the door, "Yeah?"

She walks in, and it's the woman who was ogling Jett before, right in front of me. Her admiring face has transformed to embarrassed and awkward, which means it was her who walked in on us the other night. Ha! I was hoping it was. It's all over her face that she knows her fantasy is over. He's not ever going to be hers.

Good.

Wait...what am I talking about?

I don't have any claims on him. In fact, I know we'll be saying goodbye soon. I guess I haven't given a lot of thought to what I'm going to do now that it's over and Matias is finally gone for good.

What do you do when you've fulfilled your dream?

"How are you feeling today?" she asks, carrying in the machine to check my vitals. They do this every two fucking hours. It's annoying as hell.

"Third day's a charm. Feel like my old self. Can you get the doctor for me after this?"

She turns right around to do it now. That's how uncomfortable she was. Silently laughing to myself, I gobble up some delicious, thick French fries.

"You eat like a guy, Sunshine," Jett tells me, highly entertained.

"I eat like I love food."

"And so delicately," he teases.

"Fuck being delicate." I open my empty mouth wide and take the biggest bite of burger I can fit.

He starts laughing when I realize it was too big and I can't chew it. "Ha! You remind me of my brother Jason. He's done that shit so many times!" Bending over in laughter, he hands me a napkin. "Here. Spit it out and start again."

Dr. Mackey, the one who's been checking on me for the past three days, and who performed my surgery, walks in with a smile.

"Fatburger? I'm jealous. I have to eat what's in the cafeteria."

"Oh, please," I say with an eye-roll. "Everyone knows doctors can afford the good stuff."

I pretty much shock this guy every time he sees me by saying things well-mannered – and boring – people don't say. He pauses then shrugs. "When I'm off duty, sure. But I work twenty-four hour shifts, sometimes longer. In surgeries for eight, ten hours at a time."

"Holy shit," I whisper, impressed.

He smiles. "Yeah, not able to go anywhere but downstairs and eat what's there."

Jett offers up his half-eaten burger. "Want a bite?"

Dr. Mackey laughs. "Thanks, but I just ate."

Jett smirks and chews away.

"How're you feeling?" the doctor asks me.

"I want to get out of here."

"Well..." he picks up my chart and reads, frowning like he needs glasses. "Looks good. Looks really good."

"Can I go?"

"Well, you're not being held here, Luna." He slips his hands into the enormous pockets of his lab coat.

"You're free to go at any time. We'd like to keep you here longer, to make sure your brain has healed properly."

I bring my knee up under the blanket and lean on it. "It'll heal wherever I am. It's in *my* head. Not going anywhere."

"But if you're here, we can do something if...need be."

"Like what, cut my skull open?"

On a glance to the floor, he says, "Maybe."

"Fuck that. I'd rather be out in the sun again if anything that drastic goes down. I'll take my chances, thanks."

He nods and glances from me to Jett. I look over to see Jett staring back at the doctor with a look that says, *She's the boss.* And he's got a smile on his face filled with certainty that I'm going to be fine.

Can I just admit that he's scaring the fuck out of me?

It's like he's tuned in and knows what I need.

But in my mind?

We just met five, six days ago.

He's got three months on me that I just don't have.

"I'll have them draw up the release form for you to sign, saying this is your choice, and that you won't hold us liable if something happens to you." Dr. Mackey waits for me to understand.

"Okay. Do what you have to do. I'll sign it."

"It was good meeting you, Luna." He steps closer and extends his hand. "Didn't know if I'd have the chance to."

Shaking it, I only nod. It's so crazy to have almost died and be looking at two of the men who saved your life. I know Honey Badger is included in that list. And I guess Scratch, too. Jett's told me about them, but I've yet to officially meet them. That night at the motel doesn't count.

I'll have to tell Jett to let them know I'm grateful.

Before the doctor disappears, I call after him, "Dr. Mackey!"

He leans into the room with his eyebrows up, hand on the doorframe. "Yes?"

"*Thank you.*"

He smiles. "You're welcome." He nods to Jett and holds his look a moment. He's known Jett longer than I have, too. The men silently say goodbye to each other and the doctor leaves for the last time.

"I don't know what I'm gonna do now," I say aloud, but mostly to myself.

Jett leans forward in his chair. "Come with me."

Meeting his confident eyes, I shake my head. "No, Jett."

They darken as he takes this in. "Why not?"

Because I don't know what love is.

I've never had anyone care about me like this before.

Because I'll lose you one day when you realize I'm a piece of shit, and then it'll hurt too badly.

This way I'm in control.

"Because I like to travel alone," I whisper, staring at the stupid hospital blanket.

He stands up so quickly I feel a soft wind lick my face. But I keep my eyes down because I don't want to see how much this is hurting him.

"Fuck," he mutters with pain in his deep voice. "Okay...Fine."

The sound of his feet heading for the door and then it closing brings my head up. I expected to be alone now, but there he is leaning against the wall, arms crossed, eyes locked on the tile floor. The muscles in his face are tense with confusion. "What do you do out there, Luna? How do you survive?"

I hate it when he calls me by my real name. I've gotten really used to Sunshine.

"I get by."

"How?"

"None of your business, Jett."

"Do you help or hurt?"

"What?"

He pushes off the wall, hard, and walks toward me,

unzipping his fly. I blink at him, wondering what the fuck he's doing. He yanks down the front of his pants just low enough so I can read the tattoo again.

I lift my eyes to lock with his. "Why are you showing me that now?"

"Tear 'em down to stand 'em up. That's what we do. We ride around this fuckin' country and leave it better than we found it. We do it rough, because some people need to have their face shoved into the dirt before they can stand up on their own. But when we ride away, we've changed lives."

I pull my knees up and hug myself, soaking it in. I didn't know that's what the tat meant. I mean, I kinda grasped the gist when I read it, but thought it was just something cool to have on your body. Like when people tattoo Japanese words about courage into their skin, when they're not Asian.

"Okay. What do you want me to do with this piece of information?" I ask him.

He zips and buttons his pants up, scowling at me. "When you're out there – that place you want to be alone in – do you hurt or help?"

The truth is I do both, but mostly hurt.

I shout right in his face, "I came back here to free those women!" Totally flustered at how wrong it felt to yell at him, I stammer, "I didn't know they were pregnant, but I knew they were in a hell they couldn't get out of on their own!"

Jett paces away in balled up rage. "I know about the blankets," he growls over his shoulder. "I know what you stole my credit card for."

"Then why are you standing there accusing me of being a bad person!"

"I'M SAYING YOU'RE A GOOD PERSON!" He hits the wall, then storms at me. "I'M SAYING, *JOIN US!*"

"Jett." My shoulders soften with my voice. "I don't know how to love you."

I watch his nostrils flare and his eyes widen, stunned speechless. He stares at me like he wants to make me understand something, but doesn't know the way. Fiercely rubbing his beard, he walks to the shitty bed he's been sleeping on for over three months and sits down on it, laying his head in his hands.

"I'm sorry," I whisper.

"Sunshine," he groans and lifts his head to look at me with eyes that tear me up inside. "Let me teach you."

The silence that follows kills us both.

He lays his head in his hands again and waits for me to say something.

Anything.

I just can't.

Finally after what feels like weeks, Jett rasps, the whole time staring at the floor. "Carmen needs someone with her on that train. Tonk wants her with family when that baby comes. If you don't want to be with me, I understand. I won't force you, Sunshine." He pauses and closes his eyes for a second. "But come with us as far as Louisiana. Then you can go. Ride that train with the girl. She trusts you. I trust you. And Tonk trusts you. Make sure she doesn't pop, and if she does, that she's not alone until the train's next stop."

He meets my eyes, waiting for my answer.

I owe him my life. I'm terrified of getting close to him, but I would be a real piece of shit if I said no. I want to do it. I want to help Carmen, and I want that baby to have a good start in life, because I sure didn't have one.

So I don't even hesitate. "Okay, Jett. I'll do that for you."

He nods with a beaten-down resolve, rises up and walks to the dresser where his jacket sits waiting. He stares at it before putting it on, like he's seeing a memory. "Tonk and I will ride by the train, so if anything happens we're there and ready. We'll pick a place to stop for a night because we can't make that distance without sleep." Pulling out his keys, he mutters on his way out, "I'm goin' for a ride. Need to clear my head."

Without looking back, he vanishes.

Numbly I stare after him, wishing I was a better woman.

JETT

At Alpine Texas, Tonk and I wait for the train to slow to a complete stop. More people deboard than we expected since this desert town in the western tip of Texas ain't at all that big.

Tonk's locked on finding his Carmen, standing by me like he's got crabs on his balls. "Where are they?"

"They'll be here."

"What if somethin' happened?"

"Carmen has your phone."

"Right," he grumbles, not sold.

Through a sea of much older faces we see slivers of two of the loveliest, olive skin Latinas to ever walk the planet. I grit my teeth and shove my hands in my jeans pockets. This is gonna suck.

Carmen waves and Tonk takes off running. Jealousy fires up my veins.

Fuckin' hell.

Luna watches them for a second, then glances warily to me. She just nods.

Jesus.

I want to wait where I am, but my feet have a mind of their own. I meet her in the middle. "How was the trip?"

"Good," she smiles. "She's never been on a train. Pointed out so many pretty things it kinda wore me down. You shaved your beard."

Tonk and Carmen are making out right on the platform, not caring who's watching.

I'm trying not to care, and failing.

"Yeah. It itched. What do you mean it wore you down? Like you got tired of it?"

Luna shakes her head a little, just enough for her sweet shampoo smell to torture me. "No, I mean her being so innocent and happy made me see the beauty, too, after a while."

"Ah," I huff. "Well, that's good." I reach for her backpack, but she shakes her head.

"I've got it."

"Just give me the bag."

Luna's dark eyes search me until she decides to give in. "Sorry. Not used to being around a gentleman."

"Not used to being called one." I throw it on my shoulder. and shout, "Hey lovebirds! Let's go!"

Tonk breaks the kiss and grins at me, throwing his arm around her. They slowly make their way over. "Maverick Inn?"

"Yeah."

We've been to Alpine before. With a population of just over six thousand, it's a great place to rest your head and sleep like a baby on bourbon.

At this inn we have to check in with our credit cards. No plans on doing anything worth hiding here. Tonk gets The Superior Deluxe and Carmen beams at him, stroking his forearm like it's his cock. The seventy-year-old behind the desk keeps watching, but he's really trying not to. I can tell he wishes he was young again.

My jaw tightens as I step up. "Two Deluxe rooms."

He blinks and looks at Luna, who's probably the prettiest woman he's ever seen. He steals an accidental glance at her rack and comes back to me.

"*Two* rooms?"

"Yeah."

Edgy silence. Fun times. Sharing a look with Tonk, I drop my card on the counter and wait for the guy to make snails brag about how fast they are. Fuckin' hell, man, hurry it up.

"We put a deposit on the cards to hold any costs for..."

"Yeah, I know. It's cool." Forcing a smile at Luna, I sign the receipt, and go to open the door for her. As she walks up, I mutter, "Don't even say it."

"Thank you, Jett," she whispers.

I stare after her. That's not what I thought she was gonna say.

After Carmen thanks me, too, Tonk hits my shoulder on his way out. He pauses. "Sorry, man."

"Don't."

He nods and bows his head, looking at the key. "Carmen, baby, this way."

Luna is waiting in front of the sand-colored one-story building. She follows as I head left scanning for our rooms.

The guy put us next to each other, which sucks so fuckin' bad.

A little distance would have been better, but I'd never go ask him to change it and hurt her feelings. Never in a million years.

That's not how Nancy Cocker raised me.

She raised us to be men.

Gruff, maybe.

Temperamental, fuck yes.

Pouty dickheads, *NEVER*.

"I gotta get some sleep, Sunshine. I'll see you at breakfast." Glancing over to the beautiful purple and gold sunset, I hand her the key.

"Sky sure is pretty," she quietly says as she takes it.

I nod. "Yep. Sure is." Meeting her eyes, I tell her, "But nothin's more beautiful than you."

Her mouth drops open and I turn on my weathered boot's heel for the room next door. As the key slides into the lock with ease, I remember what it felt like to slide into her. I turn the doorknob, listening for her footsteps on the hot cement, but she's still where I left her.

I don't look over.

Don't need to stick anymore glass in my heart.

LUNA

This place is definitely one of the nicer motels I've been in. Well, I guess they did call it an 'Inn,' so maybe that's the difference. Elegant Southwestern décor is how their pamphlet describes it. Big fan of the slanted wood ceilings and log bed frame. Warm and cozy.

But it's doing nothing to calm me down.

I've got ants under my skin. Red ones. That's what this feels like.

A king size bed for just me. It looks lonely.

And Jett is on the other side of the wall.

I jump at a tentative knock on the door. Grinning and relieved, I run — literally run — to answer it.

Swinging it wide, I freeze.

Carmen's eyes go big. "Oh Luna! I'm sorry. It's just me."

Ouch. "That obvious?"

She makes a face and shrugs, holding up a plastic bag. "Yeah. Can I come in?"

Stepping aside to make room for her and her belly, I shut the door and touch my forehead to it before following her to the quaint kitchen. "I had a craving for avocados so Tonk rode all over town to find me one."

"We just got here."

"Before they picked us up. Wasn't riding on the bikes fun? I've never been on one. I'm sure he didn't like going that slow."

Sighing, I tell her, "Carmen, Tonk would go two miles an hour if it made you happy. He adores you. He makes no move to hide it."

She blushes — not easy for an olive-skinned girl to do. Peeling away as she rambles on, "You and Jett were so tense and there was too much space between you."

Don't I know it. Riding on the back of his Harley and not wrapping myself around him was so, SO hard to do.

"I told you on the train, we need distance..."

"I know, but...it's just sad to me, Luna."

"Yeah, well." Crossing my arms, I watch her cut the fruit with a plastic knife. Digging out the bulbous seed with it, she hands me one half and pulls out corn tortillas. "Want me to heat them up?"

"No, this is cool."

We tear off pieces of tortilla and cut chunks of avocado to eat with them. The quiet is a comfortable one. We're used to each other now.

When we left Los Angeles and were alone together for the first time, Carmen wouldn't talk to me. Then I started telling her stories from my childhood, and she opened up. But she really is like a little bird. It doesn't surprise me that she fell for the lies, when she agreed to take 'the job.'

She was first generation American, brought over by a brother who smuggled her as a baby. When he went to jail, she had no one, and a nice white family took her in when they found the five-year-old girl on the streets. But the husband began sexually abusing her when she turned thirteen. It crushed her, of course. And her self-esteem.

She ran away when she was sixteen, but had no concept of money or how to take care of herself. One of Matias's men told her all kinds of lies to trick her. When they got her 'home,' they drugged her. Then when she got pregnant the first time, they told her she was a whore and no one would ever love her, and that the police were in on it. Her baby would go to a 'good family.' Not be raised by a whore.

That baby didn't make it.

She told me of how horrible it was for her and the others. The babies were fathered by the bodyguards, since Matias was too sick in the end to participate in his newfound commercial trafficking. And there was no structured conception. This child could be one of seven men's, she confessed. When I asked her if she told Tonk that, she nodded, which surprised me. It was when we crossed the border of Arizona into New Mexico.

She said, "He hugged me and told me he would never let anyone touch me again." Carmen stared out the window at the clay-colored mountains. "I thought you just said we were going to be in a new state now. It looks the same."

I would have smiled at her random segue and innocence, if I wasn't so sad by what she told me.

"Why aren't you staying in his room?" Carmen's brown eyes are as curious as they are patient.

To avoid the subject, I tease, "Why are you in mine?"

"Because I didn't want you lonely."

My smile fades and we eat in silence. There isn't much and it's gone too soon.

When she starts packing up, I blurt, "I thought I would be in his room." She glances up from the bag. "I...spent the last twelve hours on that train wondering how I would handle sleeping in the same room with him and keeping my heart caged up. When we were in the lobby and you looked over at me? Remember?" She slowly nods. "It was right about then that I felt maybe I'd left the hospital too soon because my heart was beating so fast it hurt in my chest. I just...when I'm around Jett I feel like I'm not close enough to him. I want to press my body to his and just stay like that."

Carmen blinks and walks to me with big arms.

"I don't need a hug," I object, stepping back.

She hesitates, but decides to ignore me. "Pretty Luna, come on."

Her belly presses into mine as her arms go around me. She rubs my back and pulls away. "He cares about you." Guessing that I'm not going to have a reply for that, she picks up the bag and heads for the door. "Tonk thinks we're having sex tonight but I'm going to have to just blow him. I feel like a big fat whale today. Baby is coming soon."

Floored, I rush over and close the door on her. "Carmen, is he making you...?"

Her eyes go huge and she shakes her head. "No! That's not what I mean!" A big smile lights her up. "He's the sexiest man, Luna. I love the sex with him. And he made me wait a long time to have it. Pissed me off." She rolls her eyes. Touching my arm, she goes soft and shy again. "Luna, when a man you want... wants to touch you for the *right* reasons, it feels really good. I'm so happy."

After she leaves, I close the door and lock it, laying my forehead on it one more time.

Glued to the thing, I hoarsely whisper, "Oh, God, this hurts!"

LUNA

Jett stares at me from under those blonde eyebrows. He's barefoot and shirtless, wearing only his jeans and as he lays his right hand on the door's frame, it's like he's bracing himself. The spidery tattoo on his chest that he and his brothers share flexes with tension.

"Sunshine, I need to get some sleep."

"I know...I just..." Glancing to the mat outside his room, I try to catch my breath. This is so scary for me, to reach out like this. "I don't want to sleep without you when you're right on the other side of the wall, Jett."

He exhales as his fingers grip the doorframe harder. "Luna, if you sleep in this room, we're gonna be fuckin' and I don't know if either of us can handle that. Unless you've changed your mind." He searches me to find out how I feel about that, and his eyes glaze over as he sees my stance hasn't changed.

"Can't we just be together now? Can't we just pretend there is no later? No future? And just be with each other?"

He frowns and releases the door, standing straight and crossing hulkish arms over his bare chest. His jeans are hanging a little, the belt not tight, and I can see the tops of the letters betraying the tat hidden below. Of course I remember what else is there, and I realize in this instant that I'm being a selfish bitch right now.

"I'm sorry," I whisper, ashamed. "I guess I'm a cunt, huh? You offered me something amazing and I can't accept it. And here I am asking you for more. Or less. Fuck," I whisper. "I don't know, Jett. I just got used to you being there when I wake up. And that's pretty crazy because I didn't know you were there when I was...gone...all those months."

"Maybe you did know," he rasps. "I talked to you every day. Wished you good morning. Talked about whatever the fuck. Explained in detail how crappy the hospital food was." He breathes deeply in and out before he adds, "And I asked you every day to stay with me. The first day I gave you permission to check out, but then I changed my mind."

I turn my head away. "You're killing me."

"I know," he rasps. "I can't fuckin' help it."

"I'll go." I head to my room. Jett reaches out and pulls me to him so quickly I gasp from surprise.

With his lips close to mine, he growls, "I'm going to regret this," and kisses me so hard it nearly bruises my lips. I press my selfish body to his.

We moan into each other's mouths because the kiss is so good. Lifting me, he slams the door with his foot, carrying me to the bed and not letting go of my mouth with the frenzied need of not being able to do this for months.

He yanks down my jeans, swearing at them when they fight back. Jett grabs me around my thighs, lifts me up and tugs the fuckers off, untying my boots and ripping my socks off. I moan as he flips me around and bends me over the bed. My panties tear under his impatience, him swearing the whole time. I tug off my shirt and my breasts fall freely because I took off my bra in my room earlier to help me breathe and calm down.

I hear him groan behind me, so I look over my shoulder and lock eyes with him. "Thank you."

A wicked smirk filled with pain and hunger tugs at the corners of his full lips. "We'll see about that." He unzips his jeans slowly, holding my gaze. "I haven't fucked anyone since I was buried deep in your hot little pussy."

"Not any of the nurses?" I tease with a naughty smile.

His eyes go hard and he leans down to grab my right nipple, pinching so hard I yelp. "You wanna play?" He begins to massage my breast. His snake is pressed into my ass cheeks and I moan at the promise of what is to come.

Jett buries his face in my neck. "Your fuckin' tits are a gift from God, Sunshine. You like my fingers on 'em?"

I moan, "Yessss."

His breathing grows rapid as he reaches down between my legs with his free hand, pulling me tight against his naked body. "Let's see if you're wet."

"If?" I croak, struck silent as his fingers slip into my swollen folds.

He touches my opening and moans right into my ear.

The heat of his breath is so yummy that my lips part wishing his tongue was sliding between them.

"Fuck, baby, you're sopping. You want me that bad, huh? But just for sex, you little slut."

"Jett!" I cry out and he bites my neck, making me moan and bend under the pressure. "That's not nice."

"Are you nice?" he chuckles and snaps my nipple between his fingers right before he grabs my hair, pulling my head up to the ceiling. I writhe under the skill of his angry fingers as he teases my clit and growls in my ear, "I'm about to make you forget other men exist."

As he shoves his index and middle finger into my hole, I moan, "Cocky bastard..." He's stroking me as he massages my neck with his teeth, gnawing on me in the beat of those fingers. My back is arched. The ceiling is above me, and it's all I can see.

He's got complete mastery of my body and I fight the climax, angry at him for owning me like this.

Because I know he's right.

I will never have another man inside my body and not think of Jett Cocker.

"Oh God," I whisper as the burning tingles turn to flames.

"That's it. Cum for me, baby," he moans in my ear, panting in time with me.

"No," I whisper, struggling against giving in.

"Let me in, baby. Let all that pain go."

I cry out as he starts lightly flicking my clit with his thumb while his fingers penetrate me in swift sure pumps. Dynamite explodes in my veins and I scream, "I FUCKING HATE YOU!"

Jett ignores me and pulls my head back to kiss me hard. My tongue reaches for his first, desperate to taste him. I'm cumming all over his hand. Bucking under the pleasure. Letting go of the fight. I bite his lip as he pulls back to look at me. He smirks and growls, "Little bitch. I still can't believe you stole my credit card."

"I'd do it again," I shoot back with a smirk of my own.

He laughs loudly and then shoves my torso down, lifting my ass and snarling, "Fucking look at this thing here. Sweet holy fuck, look at your ass!"

He gives it a slap and rubs his cock's blunt tip against my wet pussy. I moan hard and rasp, "Oh God, you feel so good."

He dives in, filling my starving pussy with a meal. We moan together and he rakes short fingernails down my spine, smacking my ass cheeks again as he begins to stroke himself inside me.

I am trembling at his size. This is pleasure mixed with pain. It's been months. But do I mind? Fuck no. It feels way better than it hurts.

"I'm gonna fill you to the rim, baby."

For some reason he stops abruptly.

"What's wrong?" Flinging my hair back, I look over my shoulder to see why he stopped.

Frowning really hard, he pulls out of me and flips me around, his naked body climbing onto mine, cock dripping along the way. "Luna, I'm not gettin' you pregnant against your will. I know I didn't use protection back in the motel, but things are different after that mansion, and what we saw. I'm not one of those fuckin' animals."

Pain twists my chest into pieces and I shake my head. "I know you're not!"

"If you got pregnant, Luna, there'd be no getting rid of me. Understand? I'd never be some deadbeat dad, and I've got no fuckin' condoms with me. I almost bought some but knew it would be too tempting to break your door down if I did."

"Jett, I don't think I can get pregnant, it's okay."

His frown deepens. "What do you mean?"

"I've never been, and I had these polyps, and I don't know..." I whisper, feeling vulnerable suddenly. This kind of talking is way more intimate than hard fucking, that's for sure. "I heard from this gypsy woman that I'd never conceive."

He snarls, "What the fuck?" protectively, like he'd beat the woman up if she were here, for saying such a thing to me.

"No, she was a good person. I stayed with her for a while when I was a teenager. She said it one night like she was having a vision. *The things you saw as a child closed your womb for good, and for protection.* I never told her about any of it! But she knew somehow...so I believed her. I don't think I can have kids. I've come to terms with it. It's okay."

Jett stares at me, his features hard, like he doesn't

know what to do with this and doesn't believe it. "You're willin' to chance it?"

He's going to be a dad someday. It's so obvious in how loyal he is by nature. With his Ciphers and his family. And how he's been here for me, a stranger who was mortally wounded and all alone.

"I really don't think it's a possibility, Jett. I'm sorry. It's another reason I'm not a good woman for you to stay with."

"What if you got pregnant?" He leans down and takes my mouth for a ride. Gasping away from me, he stares into my eyes, "What about then?"

"Jeez, what a kiss!"

"Would you abort it?"

"The miracle baby?" I ask with a sad smile. "No, of course not! But this is a stupid conversation we really don't need to be thinking about. Never gonna happen."

A grin spreads his moist lips.

"What?" I demand. "Why are you smiling like that?"

"Because you said that once before." He kisses me again and I return it with equal passion, remembering when he followed me out of the diner.

Never gonna happen turned into fucking him in that motel room the same night.

I can't lie that I wish I could have children. That

woman's words burned loss into my soul and I've held onto that prediction.

Jett wants to get me pregnant. Well, if he succeeds, I guess I'll have to take it as a sign I should be here in his arms. They feel so good, so right, so unforgettable.

He moves us up the bed by lifting and tossing me, then throws my legs over his shoulders and dives that gorgeous cock inside. We moan and he digs into my hips with both hands, manipulating me for our mutual pleasure. Watching my face as he fucks me, he whispers, "Gonna give it my best shot."

"Jett!" I cry out, covering my face with my hands as the shattering begins, my pussy throbbing and clenching and cumming so hard.

He massages my breasts, bending his huge back so he can lick my nipples, biting and teasing them. He growls into that tender flesh and lets my legs fall, turning me over and lifting me so that I'm on my knees. I slam my hands onto the headboard of wooden logs and grip onto them as he enters me roughly from behind.

Smiling at him over my shoulder I whisper, "My poor little pussy."

He grins as pleasure attacks his core. I watch him look down and drink in how great my ass looks slamming against his pelvic bone. He slips his thumb into my ass cheeks and touches my anus, holding there and shocking me. I can't help but moan.

He pounds harder, filling me, ripping me right down the middle. Oh God, he buries himself to the hilt and swells up with a burning explosion I can't wait to feel. He roars and all the veins in his muscles contract as he shoots his hot semen inside me. I scream as I join him, gritting my teeth as the brilliant fire clenches my walls around him time and again.

"Holy Fuck!" Jett roars, "Sunshine! I'm cumming harder than I ever have, baby."

Trembling and holding onto the headboard, I whimper his name incoherently. He wraps an arm around my stomach and collapses in a thrusting mess of instinct.

When we calm, the only sound in the room is gasps for air. He pulls me to lie down and buries his face in my breasts, half lying on me with one heavy leg over both of mine. Jett kisses them all over, taking his time. He rises up, teasing my tongue, lacing it with his own. Our lips move so easily together. Everything is smooth.

It's quiet in my soul right now.

I can think about tomorrow later.

He falls back onto the pillow and exhales loudly, staring at the ceiling. Our hands find each other and entwine. "You wanna go to a wedding?"

I glance over at him. "What? No. I hate weddings."

He chuckles and throws his other arm behind his head, resting on his hand. His body is glistening. "That's what I figured."

I was about to say, *who're the idiots,* but I hold my tongue. "Who's getting married?"

"My brother Jake."

Oof.

Um...no way.

Meeting the whole Cocker family? All those brothers and his parents, who have got to be still together from what I've learned about who Jett is. Even as a biker this guy's got commitment all over him. I bet he has no idea of that, though.

I release his hand so I can roll over and lie on him. "I'm not the type you bring home to parents."

He blinks at me like he's deciding what to say to that. His eyebrows rise up and he mutters, "I'm not the type of guy you bring home to my dad, so we have that in common."

"What do you mean?"

He sighs. "We don't get along."

"Is he an asshole?"

"Eh...asshole? Sometimes, yeah. But he's a hypocrite for sure. That's his main flaw. My dad's a congressman." Jett glances to me for my reaction.

"Wow," I whisper.

"Yeah. He doesn't like having a son who fights the

system." Shifting his gaze back up I watch turbulence run through his features. "But he had me come to the rescue of Jake just last year. Because he couldn't do anything about the situation...he needed me to do my thing. Fuckin' asshole."

"What'd you do?"

In brief detail Jett tells me about it. I listen with the returning sense that this guy is too good for me. I don't deserve him. I know that as much as I know my own name. And it isn't Sunshine, no matter what he sees.

"I knew he wouldn't thank me or anything," Jett finishes, pulling me up for a kiss. "And he didn't."

"How long has it been since you've seen him?"

Jett thinks about it a second. "Four years."

"Your brothers, too!?"

"Nah. I see them every few months or so. The longest I didn't was six months. Our house – not my brothers...the Ciphers' House – it's outside New Orleans. Really beautiful and peaceful there. South Vacherie, Louisiana. I hope you get a chance to see it."

I bite my lips and watch him look at me.

He smiles. "You look so fuckin' scared sometimes, Sunshine. It's pretty funny."

I dryly shoot back, "Oh yeah, it's hilarious."

He laughs and adjusts his gorgeous body, bending his knee and pulling me closer. We claim each other's mouths in a deep kiss that we feel everywhere. It's long and slow and never picks up speed. His cock fills up and presses against my thigh and I moan into his lips at the welcome feeling.

He smiles when we separate and looks at me like I'm the most beautiful woman he's seen in his whole life.

I've never cared what a man thought about my looks, but when Jett gazes at me like this, it's a little bewitching — I forget anything exists besides us.

He's locked on me like he's made for me or something.

"JETT!" Tonk shouts through the door as he bangs on it with his fist. "JETT!!"

We rise up with a start. "YEAH?" he calls back, jumping off the bed. "Somethin's wrong," he mutters to me.

"SHE'S IN LABOR, JETT. HOLY FUCK – GET OUT HERE! I'M FUCKIN' TERRIFIED!"

We rush to put our clothes on and Jett swears at his erection, "Shit, go down!" shoving it into his jeans and belting them up with intense discomfort.

"COMING!" I call out.

"LUNA?!!" Tonk shouts. And in a quieter voice, we hear him say, "Well, I'll be."

In no time we're heading for their room, Tonk just in boxer briefs.

As the three of us storm inside, I quickly take it all

in. The room is beautiful – totally deserves the name Deluxe. Poor nineteen-year-old Carmen is on the bed grimacing and holding onto her big belly through the blankets which she's got pulled modestly over her naked body.

"She told me she didn't want to fuck and then she fuckin' climbed on top of me and said she changed her mind!"

"I couldn't help it," Carmen cries out. "I love him!"

"What was I supposed to do?" Tonk desperately demands of Jett. "I COULDN'T SAY NO!"

"I know the feelin,'" Jett mutters, pulling out his phone from his jeans. We exchange a look as I hold Carmen's hand. "Yes," he says to the person on the other side. "We need an ambulance. A woman's gone into labor." He listens for a moment, says, "We're at the Maverick Inn." He pauses. "Okay, thanks." As he hangs it up, he walks to the bed, with Tonk right there, needing the support of the older Cipher.

"You ever seen a woman have a baby, Jett?" he asks.

"Nah. Now's as good a time as any," he grins, swatting his buddy on his back. "Probably should put some clothes on."

Jett turns to face a wall while I help Carmen into a long skirt and cotton blouse she and Tonk bought on the Santa Monica Pier while they were getting to know each other. She didn't have any clothes and he stepped up and changed that.

When we were spending those few days and nights together in Cedars Sinai Hospital, Jett told me the Ciphers have money. They take it from evil pricks they save people from, and some is donated by people and organizations who want to thank them. Their club isn't new. He's third generation. The president is in his eighties. Some men have come and gone, some didn't like the 'do-gooder bullshit,' he explained. There were three factions set across the states, but it was growing in numbers. Ten men called Louisiana home and traveled from there rarely staying long.

And with Carmen giving birth right now, I probably won't be seeing it after all, since she is the reason I haven't run away.

JETT

You'd think no one ever had a kid before, by how Tonk and I are pacing the hospital. This place is so much smaller than the one in Beverly Hills, and it's driving him insane like he's not sure they're up for the job. He keeps asking if she's gonna be okay, to anyone who walks by. He must've asked me a thousand times, clutching my arm each time.

Luna's the only calm person here, sitting over there on one of the black polyester chairs by the wall, staring off and biting her lips.

She and I keep glancing to each other, both of us wishing she was in there with the girl. She'd asked to be, but the baby was breach, and had to come out with a C-section. They put Carmen out and explained to

Luna that cutting her stomach would be far less easy to watch than a normal birth. They don't allow an audience for that here because too many people faint.

She tried to argue, but it was policy.

Finally a silver-haired male obstetrician pushes open the double doors and heads for us. Tonk jumps and turns midair, rushing over like something out of a fuckin' cartoon. "She okay?"

He nods, looking tired. He was on call, and Tonk's been driving him a little crazy. "She is. She's sleeping. Your baby is healthy." He pauses with a smile in his eyes. "It's a girl."

Tonk's arm flies back, reaching for me and I stride quickly over to grab his forearm. "A girl," he whispers, so excited you'd think it really *was* his.

"You can see her in the window. They're bathing her now."

"Fuck yeah! Lead me to her!" he cries out, making the doctor smile.

Luna joins us and we all follow the man to where about ten beds lie, empty all but two, on the other side of thick, spotless glass. One tiny crib has a baby in it so small it doesn't look real.

"What's wrong with that one?" I ask the doc, nervous about what he's gonna say.

"Oh, he just came early, that's all. We're watching him closely. He'll be fine." The doctor excuses himself and we all stare at the crimson creature Tonk is gonna raise, watching in silence as two nurses swaddle her up. We missed the bath.

"I guess they move quickly," Tonk mutters with disappointment.

"They want to get her warm again," Luna reassures him, smiling at the infant. "You're a good person, Tonk, to raise that baby."

"She's mine now. Mine and Carmen's. And that's all she's ever gonna know."

Luna crosses her arms like she's cold. I put my arm around her and she leans into me. Staring at that little human – who looks like an alien, if anyone asked me – I picture Luna's face as she told me she can't get knocked up. She was really confident it was true, but I saw the sadness she hid there.

I tighten my hold on her and kiss the top of her half-shaved head. "Lemme talk to Tonk a minute."

Her dark eyes drift up and she nods. I plant a quick kiss on her lips that surprises her but she doesn't back away. "I'll be in the waiting room, 'kay?" I nod. As she heads off I swat her butt. She yelps and grins over her shoulder. "Nice steal."

"Nice ass," I smirk.

When the sound of her footsteps fades against the closing of the double doors, I exhale. "I need you to do me a favor."

"You got it," he says, eyes locked on the baby. "Look at her little face, Jett. Can you believe she was gonna be sold off to some stranger?"

"No, I can't. It's foul. Let it go."

He nods. "Yeah. After today. It's just too much of a miracle that this has happened to me, man. You know my father..." he glances over and checks himself. "Oh, no you don't. It was Scratch I told. Well, my dad's an asshole, Jett. I'm not gonna be like him. I'm gonna show that little girl and her mother that I'm a good man they can trust with their fuckin' lives. You hear me?" He looks at me like he's challenging me to dispute this.

"I have no doubt."

He stares at me for a charged beat then nods, turning back to the window.

"So, this favor..."

"Yeah," he mumbles, admiring the sleeping child as the nurse tends to the tiny boy lying beside her crib.

"I need you to loan me your bike."

Tonk's head jerks back to me. "What?!"

"Look, you're not gonna wanna leave them in some train, even with Luna. Not because it isn't safe but because you'll be fuckin' miserable. It'll be the first ride where you want your bike in a ditch, so you can be with your women."

At hearing me use the plural, he huffs, waiting. "Okay...go on."

"Luna and I will ride the bikes back to South Vacherie."

A deep frown shoots into his forehead and he's about to object when he turns to look at the baby girl again. "Fuck," he mutters.

"If she drops it, I'll have it repaired. I need more time with her."

Side-eyeballing me, he grumbles, "Jesus, Jett, those months watching her breathe on a fuckin' machine really got to you, didn't they?"

"She got to me before that. Just like that Mexican flower had you wrapped around her finger the second she clung to you in that fuckin' dungeon. I saw it on your face. Didn't surprise me at all you claimed her."

"Well, it surprised me."

We both face the window. After a while, I confess, "You're younger than me. I've been around. Had my fill. I know myself."

"You've never fucked a girl longer than a week, Jett. Not that I've seen."

"Have any of us?"

"It's my bike, man. My fuckin' baby."

"That's your baby, too." I knock his shoulder with mine. "Tonk, she's gonna leave me again. I can feel it." He meets my eyes. "This one's it, man. She's *it* for me. I can't let her go."

I watch his profile as he mulls it over. "I never thought I'd say this, but okay. Take the bike."

Now how am I gonna talk Luna into it...

Just gotta keep her with me a little longer.

She's gotta fall for me.

She's gonna fall for me.

I have to believe that.

LUNA

Itchy. That's how I feel. I don't know what's happening next. I feel like I should take off right after I tell Carmen her baby is beautiful, and of course make sure she sees my face and knows I care.

But then I should go.

Because I don't want to. And that's a good enough reason right there.

These people are getting too close to me. I can't even think about Jett without imagining touching him. When he put his arm around me as we stared at that adorable newborn, I was way too comfortable.

What's really scaring me is the growing belief I can trust him. That he deserves trust.

The second he appears through the double doors,

my heart stops just at the sight of him. His face is serious. "Let's get some food."

I'm here with my arms tightly crossed like a shield. He acts like he can't see I'm itching, but that's an act. He's at the electric exit leaving the wake of their *whoosh* behind him as he heads out.

Didn't give me a chance to object.

Smart man.

Too smart.

"I should be moving on," I call after him as I follow.

I told my feet to stay in the waiting room, so I could see Carmen quickly, then hitch a ride somewhere far away. Did they listen? No. My body wants to be with him. My heart says no fucking way am I leaving. *You want to kill me?*

Jett mounts his bike with sensual ease and glances over as he hits the cushion behind his perfect ass. "Get on."

"Jett..."

Grey eyes lock on me and narrow with purpose. "I need one more favor from you, Sunshine, then you can go. I'm not gonna stop you. I promise."

"What's the favor?"

"Get on."

Huffing, I grab his shoulders and step onto the footrest to swing my leg over and mount the rumbling beast. As I strap on the helmet, I tell myself I'm just going to lightly hold onto his waist for this ride – and keep my distance – but again my body has other ideas. Before I know it, I'm pressed against his back as tightly as I can be, with my arms wrapped around his mammoth torso, fingers tucked into his unzipped leather jacket, stroking his gorgeous chest and abs. He makes a guttural noise that says he loves this.

I am a glutton for punishment.

Tucking into him I watch eight-foot-tall cactus trees whiz by. At Penny's Diner on the US 90, he gruffly tells me to wait with the bike. Biting my lips, I watch him stroll inside the silver building they designed with an Airstream trailer in mind.

How am I going to say goodbye to him? What's the best way?

Just disappear and get it over with.

I can't do that.

You did it before.

Yeah, but I was focused on saving those women.

It'll be easier for him if you just leave. Then he can call you a cunt for the rest of his life.

True.

Running my fingers over the gas tank, I glance behind me to the diner and watch the waitress smiling up a storm as Jett hands her some cash. Jesus, does she have to stick her tits out that much?

When you leave, he'll be fucking anybody he

wants...for the rest of his life.

"Shut up!" I mutter aloud, leaning on his beast and crossing my arms. As he strolls into the sunlight, I call over, "Why didn't we just eat inside?"

"We will." He throws me a devilishly handsome smile and hands me the bag. "You're gonna have to feel this up during the ride."

Chuckling, I shoot back, "Fuck you."

"You like these abs, don't you, Sunshine?" He pulls up his shirt and shows them off.

Yes, I do. Damn he is fucking hot.

"Nope, was just trying to figure out if you'd gained some weight, Jett."

He laughs outright. "Sure you were."

Back at the Maverick Inn, he walks to his room and unlocks the door. We haven't said a word since teasing each other back there, but I have been humming all over since he said we were going to eat inside, because he laced that statement with sexual innuendo. If he just meant eggs and orange juice on the table in here, I'll be disappointed.

Fuck, I really am a selfish bitch.

"What'd you get us?"

"Breakfast." He sets the Styrofoam boxes out and unwraps plastic silverware. "We've been up all night. Tired?"

"Yeah. You?"

He shrugs. "Feelin' pretty awake, surprisin'ly."

I had no idea how hungry I was until the bacon touched my tongue. It's the best invention ever, first of all, but when you've spent hours fucking and then more hours waiting for a baby – and all the emotional energy they both use up – food never tasted quite so good.

More than once I catch Jett smiling at my lack of femininity. I scarf the hell out of this food without reservation or shame. He's no different.

Finally able to speak, I gulp down O.J. and ask, "What's this favor?"

"We'll talk about it after this." He rises up and yanks my chair away from the table.

"What are you doing?"

"Eating." My pants are unzipped faster than you can say cock and he yanks them down and buries his tongue in my surprised pussy.

"I haven't bathed, Jett!"

He murmurs into my cunt, "I could give a shit," and starts licking away. "You taste like us, baby. Ripe and fuckin' delicious." I get yanked forward and he's practically lying on his stomach, one jean-covered leg bent, the other sprawled out. His ass looks phenomenal, and his tongue feels even better. I moan and hold his head, lacing my fingers into his hair, but letting him find the way because he needs no GPS for my body.

Every crevice is explored and he groans into my sensitive pussy walls, making me boneless as I moan his name over and over. He growls between tight little flicks on my clit, "Cum on my tongue...I can feel you aching to."

"I'm so close!"

He switches sides of my clit and teases me until I scream. My thighs grip his head in a vice I can't stop. "Oh God!" I cry out, trembling.

Whimpering, I'm lifted off the chair and carried to the bed. He slides my shirt off and takes off his clothes, staring at my hooded eyes with white-hot lust in his. Naked and gorgeous he climbs on top of me and I grab his cock and stroke it. He groans and kisses my breasts as I pull on his shaft, rasping, "Jett, fuck me."

I stop myself from saying, *one last time.*

He locks his mouth onto mine. He's right about the taste. It's salty. It's dirty. And I love it. All of me reacts as he teases my nipples. He's rock hard in my hand. He grabs my hand off, yanks my arms over my head and pushes my knees up, positioning himself and pressing in with a long, sure, growling thrust. My back arches as I let out a long moan. He drives into me over and again. Tearing me apart. Devouring me with kisses that cover everything he can reach. "Fuck Sunshine, I want to cum you feel so good."

"Do it," I rasp. "It's safe."

He chuckles like he thinks I'm crazy, then his beautiful grey eyes lock onto me and harden. He grimaces and I thought he felt good pounding my cunt like this. But it gets so much better when he cums, swelling and working harder like he has no more control.

My jaw clenches.

His balls punch my ass cheeks harder and harder as he loses his fucking mind.

"HOLY SHIT!" he shouts.

He pulls my body off the bed as he holds inside of me, spilling his heat inside of me. I can't stop begging for it to never stop.

"Jett, I..." Closing my eyes I shut up. I can't believe I almost said, *I love you.* I've only ever said it to my mother and that was a long time ago.

Stunned by my own feelings, I stay quiet as he falls on top of me and kisses me hard, pumping every last juicy bit inside my bruised pussy. We hold each other as he gasps for air and rises up to look at me. "Ride with me to South Vacherie. Tonk needs someone to get his bike back home."

He gives me no time to react before he buries his handsome face in my neck and sucks on me, leaving behind a cherry red mark that will serve as a reminder of him when I am gone.

I'm kidding myself if I think it won't hurt like a motherfucker leaving him behind. I'm in deep now.

He's marked more than my skin, he's branded my heart with the name *Jett Cocker*.

JETT

After some much needed sleep, Sunshine agrees to a shower with me. And when I start to soap her up so I can watch the bubbles drift and pop over her amazing tits, she lets me.

I expected a fight.

I can do it...stuff like that.

But Sunshine says nothing as the suds slide down curves I can't stop caressing. We kiss in the sunbeams that slice into the steamy air. She watches me soap myself up last. "You're not gonna help?" I joke, but I can tell she's getting off on watching.

She reaches over and grabs my cock. "I'll clean this right here."

Grinning, I step a little closer. "Be my guest."

"Well, give me the bar," she smiles with a challenge in her sultry brown eyes.

"Fuck, that feels good." I've been hard since we stepped in. Hell, I've been hard since she didn't argue about driving with me back home. Not that she's given me an answer yet. But I have a feeling it's yes.

This is my last ditch effort to imprint myself on the woman. All of this. I want her to change her mind. I want her to want me as much as I want her.

"Sunshine, you're pretty fuckin' good at this," I groan as I sway under her skill.

"I'm just watching your face and doing more of what makes you frown like that."

"I'm frowning?"

"Pleasure-frowning. You're making this amazing sex face, Jett." She takes my kiss with passion and our tongues lash around as the ache in my cock throbs harder. "You want this?" Sunshine lets go and turns around, arching her gorgeous ass in the air.

"Go slow at first. I'm a little sore."

Rinsing off the soap with a quick flash under the hot streaming water, I grab onto her ass, inching my length into her pussy a little at a time. She rises on her toes and moans. I could listen to this woman make that noise for the rest of my life.

Tonk's right. I've never been with anyone longer than a week, because they can't hold my attention.

I need a wild feral cat like Luna, in my life. Never knew it 'til I met her. I just saw myself being alone and ridin' alone until I died. Flings, but nothin' more.

When women begged me to stay it was never hard to say no. I've seen more than my fair share of tears. But I never cried for any of them. *I'm not the one for you baby,* I'd tell them. *If I stick around any longer it'll just be harder to let me go. And your man's waitin' for you.*

They never believed me when I said that, but I meant that shit.

I knew I wasn't the one.

I'd just be taking his place by sticking around.

But fuck, the crying always tore me up.

My mom raised me to do right by women.

I try my best. I don't succeed often.

And now look at me – fucking this wild, gorgeous thing who makes me laugh at the weirdest moments, with everything I have just to make her body go limp so her heart follows.

I'm a desperate sonofabitch.

I see the look she's never lost.

She's leavin' the first chance she gets.

Her hands crawl up the tile as she cries out, her pussy trembling around the base of my cock as I drive it in deep. "Jett," she moans, driving me insane with how sexy she said it.

I bend my knees deeper and ram her until there's nothing left for me to give. Our wet bodies are matted to each other as steam wafts around our heads. I kiss her shoulder blades and whisper into her slippery, olive skin, "I love you."

Her body goes tense in my arms. "Jett..." she rasps.

"No," I murmur into her ear. "You don't have to say anything. It's okay. Just...shhhh."

She's panting and I slide out of her and turn her around, water cascading between us.

"Luna, I want you. Only you. But I know what you've been through and I know it will take time for you to believe my heart is true. That I'm a good man."

With a pained look twisting her all up, she whispers, "I'm not a good woman, Jett."

"The fuck you aren't." I grab the back of her head and kiss her deeply. She fights me but finally gives in, slipping her arms around my neck. My cock twitches like it can go another round and she feels it against her.

"We should see if Carmen's okay," she whispers against my lips.

I stare at her and see the wall.

The decision's been made.

She's dead set on being on her own.

"You're sayin' no, aren't you?"

With tears in her eyes, she nods. "I have to."

Reaching over, I turn off the faucet.

I didn't win. I just made myself look like a fool.

I'm not gonna beg. Every time she rejects me, it's like a scorpion's sting.

"Right. Let's go."

The hospital's busier than we left it. Luna and I ask for Carmen's room and get directed to it. Like I've got O.C.D. I keep replaying my telling her, *I love you.*

I hold the door for her and call in, "Everyone decent?"

"Fuck yeah! Get in here!" Tonk calls back with a smile in his deep voice. "Look what I found." He holds up his baby girl. Swaddled in a pale pink blanket, she sleeps in his arms. Since he's like a giant, she looks extra tiny and fragile.

"Your arms are as big as her body," Luna smiles, staring down at the little thing. She touches the baby's forehead and then goes to Carmen. "How are you?"

"So happy!" They talk about what's been happening since we left, but I tune it out.

Tonk glances up like looking at this little girl is the only thing that matters. But then he sees my face. I'm doing my best to look normal, but man-to-man...he sees it. His eyes darken and his eyebrows cock up. Silently I nod, letting him know he's reading it right. There is no happy ending for me.

Then Carmen says something that's interesting

enough to grab my attention. "Will I see you at the house, Luna? Please!?"

Luna blinks quickly to me and sees me watching. It's not subtle how quiet the room just got.

So I rescue her, because...I'm not a dick, that's why. "She's got some things she wants to do on her own, Carmen. This is goodbye."

"At least for now," Luna tells the young girl who looks at her like a hero. "I'll get Tonk's phone number and call you all the time. We'll still be friends, okay?"

Carmen is crushed but she nods before she steals a worried look at me. "I wish you'd stay, Luna. I won't know anyone."

"You'll have me, baby," Tonk tells her as he walks to the other side of the bed with their daughter. "And you'll have Celia."

Carmen reaches for her baby, smiling at her sleeping face. "We named her after my grandmother."

"It's a beautiful name, Carmen. I love it," Luna smiles. She leans in to see the baby and reaches gently to touch her forehead again. "She's so..." The words trail off and she rises up and turns away.

Tonk exchanges a look with me. Carmen's too young to know that Luna just got a little jealous.

I could punch that fuckin' gypsy in the mouth for what she said to her.

And the thought of another man proving it wrong is too much for me to stomach.

"Let's get on the road."

Tonk stiffens, then pulls out his keys. "You know how to ride?" he asks her.

I'm half-expecting her to turn me down and say she's not gonna do it. But she nods. "Yup."

It's a long pause as he holds the keys over her open, waiting palm.

"Tonk."

He frowns at me. "Alright. Fuck." Then drops them.

Luna's fingers wrap protectively around them and she reassures my fellow Cipher, "You've got nothing to worry about." Turning to Carmen, she leans in and gives an awkward hug. "How long before you get to go home?"

"Two days. They need to make sure the cut in my stomach is healing."

Luna nods. "Have fun on the train ride you guys." Our arms brush as she passes me and she glances up at the contact like she felt the same shock I did. "Ready?" she whispers.

I clasp arms with Tonk and silently thank him for his sacrifice before I give a wink to his future bride. "Glad this worked out for you guys."

Carmen watches Luna leave and I can tell she wants to tell me something, so I linger for a second.

On a sweet smile, the new mom whispers, "Don't give up."

Her thighs are barely touching mine and she's holding onto my waist on the ride back to the Inn to get our things, Tonk's Harley, and take off.

She was fuckin' wrapped around me on the ride here.

I'm getting the message.

We collect our things in our own rooms and while I have a minute to myself, I walk over to the open front door and shut it. Pulling out my phone I call Scratch.

"'Bout fuckin' time you checked in," he grumbles.

"Carmen had a baby girl."

"Holy shit." He lets out a long whistle. "How's Tonk?"

"Lovin' every second."

Scratch tells me in his deep vibrato, "Finally gets to have the family he's always wanted. You coming home now?"

"That's what I called to tell you. Yeah." The bed stares back at me with images cutting into my head of Luna and I lying on each other. "Just me and Luna for now. Tonk's takin' the train back with the baby – Celia – so we should be pulling in tomorrow at the latest."

"Luna's comin' with ya? Guess all that waitin'

around paid off."

"She's not stayin,' Scratch. Just helpin' me with Tonk's ride."

Scratch is quiet for a second and I hear Led Zeppelin playing in the background, really far away. But I'd know that awesome shit anywhere. "How you feel about that, Jett?"

"I'm a man. I don't feel."

He chuckles. "Right. What was I thinkin'?"

Grabbing my toothbrush, sounds of her moaning in the shower haunt my eardrums so I make quick strides to get the hell out of here. "I tried to talk her into stayin.' No go."

After more of just the distant record playing, finally Scratch somberly confesses, "I had a woman say no once."

"Did she change her mind?" I'm not sure if he's talking about Mona, his current wife.

"Nah, she stuck to it. I'll never forget her. Laura. Fuck, what a broad she was. Beautiful little tornado from hell but I sure did love her."

We hang up with me feelin' shittier. Walking into dusk I find Luna already at the bikes, ready to go.

"I heard you on the phone."

I tense like a rattlesnake in danger. "What'd you hear?"

"Nothing," she quickly says. "Just heard your

voice. Muffled. Why? You have something to hide?"

Shit motherfucker sonofabitch. She has to go and test me. I have to be honest with her. The one thing this woman needs more than anything is for me to be trustworthy.

Which is a bitch and a half.

We all tell white lies.

"Nothin' to hide, Sunshine. I told Scratch what I already told you – that I wanted you to stay. Not fun walking through the rejection all over again."

Firing up out of nowhere, Luna's dark eyes flash. "I'm not rejecting you! I just can't give you what you want!"

"Oh really – we're gonna do this now? Fine. Let's fuckin' go. You could *try*, Sunshine," I growl, leaning into her face.

She rises up on her toes to meet my anger with equality. "I've given you a lot already! I'm here aren't I?"

"Shit, well, don't do me any favors, babe." I turn and toss my shit in the saddlebags.

She rounds my bike so we're face to face over the back of it. "I didn't ask you to sit by me in the hospital."

Laughing under my breath, I shake my head. "No, you didn't. You couldn't really do that...since YOU WERE IN A COMA!"

"My point exactly! I didn't have the time you had

to get all worked up with feelings!" Her lips go tight and I swear I've never punched a woman but in this split second I have to remind myself of that.

"Sunshine!" I jab my index finger at her. "You're fuckin' lyin' to yourself if you think you don't care about me. I see it. Hide it all you want, but I see things you don't even know you're feelin.' This fight you're pickin' with me right now is just because we're gonna say goodbye in less than twenty-four hours and this makes you feel better about that. This way you'll be able to call me an asshole and pretend you're NOT fallin' in love with me. Well, I hate to break the fuckin' news, but YOU ARE."

Her eyes are wide. She's speechless. Good. I can't take this bullshit where someone is that out of touch with themselves. I know she's feral. I know her family sucked worse than most. Who she spent her years with after she left that whorehouse, probably wasn't any kind of stable environment. The bullshit gypsy prediction about her ovaries is sign enough.

"You know how to ride?" I growl, handing her the keys.

"No," she admits through gritted teeth.

"Fuck," I mutter, glaring at her. "You lied. Great."

"I told you I'm not a good woman," she spits at me.

"BAD WOMEN DON'T BUY A VAN FULL OF FUCKIN' COMFORTERS!"

Luna's lips part as her eyes go soft.

Do I have to remind her that she doesn't suck?

I guess so.

"You know what else bad women don't do, Sunshine?" I lean over my bike and hold her resistant gaze. "They don't inspire the admiration of the Carmens of the world. You see how that girl looks at you? If you were a fuckin' cunt to her on that train, she wouldn't be like that. I'm guessing you treated her like a little sister and took her in *here*." I punch my chest. "And bad women don't make men like me want to be by their side for FUCKIN' EVER." I walk around the bike, grab her by her shoulders so that she's on her tiptoes. In a lower voice I inform her without even taking a breath, "You come from a fucked-up family. I get it. I do. You think you're evil because that man was your dad, but your mom got tricked. And she was good. Her blood pumps through your veins, Luna! My mother told me to hold out for a different kind of woman. And by different, she didn't mean an asshole. She meant one who makes me happy. And I wouldn't think that was you if I had any belief – any at all – that you were a piece of shit." I set her down and lift her chin, looking down into her wounded eyes. "The only one who thinks you're a piece of shit here, is you."

Sunshine stares at me as I walk to Tonk's bike and motion for her to join me. "This is how you ride."

LUNA

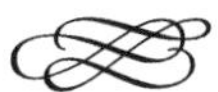

I'm uh...I can't even...think.

Jett shows me that the left handle is the clutch, the right is the gas. The brakes are on both, they just have to be pulled, one for the front tire, the other for the rear.

"This lever is how you shift," he instructs me as he points to the small footrest right in front of the one my left foot rests on. "You ever drive a stick?"

I stare at him for a second. "Uh...yes."

"You lying?"

"No," I whisper, shaking my head a little.

Those things he just said are ringing. But I don't want to drop Tonk's bike after I lied to his face. And I don't want to die.

Well, maybe I do a little.

After what Jett Cocker just slapped into my core, I am overwhelmed and scared shitless. Seeing a mirror up this close to your psyche isn't fun.

"Okay, so you know how you use a clutch in that? It's the same here."

I nod, trying to focus. "So I hold the clutch down and then pump the pedal to shift."

"Yeah, and to switch up gears, put your foot under it and push up, one at a time. It's a heavy pedal – this is a Harley so everything is heavy and powerful – you won't be able to upshift easily anyway. But just be careful. We'll take it nice and slow."

"How long is the drive?"

Did I really just *squeak?*

Running my hands over the part of my hair that's growing back, I look at him and try to act like I'm calm.

I'm anything but calm.

And he knows. This man knows me way better than I do.

Thinking for a second, he glances away. I watch his brain computing the distance. "About twelve hours. We'll have to stop and sleep."

"No, I can make it," I quickly say.

He regards me with impatience and crosses his arms. "The Ciphers can make it because we're conditioned to, but you my dear ain't gonna fuckin' make that drive without exhaustion. And I'm not risking your life because you're scared of sleeping with me again and admitting how you feel."

"Jesus Jett. You're so smart, aren't you?"

He nods. "Cocky, too. And you can take that sarcasm and shove it, Kitten. I'm not a fan."

I shout, "God!" as he walks to his bike and opens his saddlebag again with his back to me. "You are infuriating!"

"We've got somethin' in common," he mutters, then tosses me a sweater. "Put this on under your jacket." He buckles up the bag again and gets on his bike, putting on his riding glasses and helmet.

I'm so pissed off – mostly at myself and partly at him for being psychic or something – that I don't feel afraid as I mount Tonk's bike, and tear my jacket off. Pulling the sweater over my head, Jett and I exchange a heated, angry look.

"Tonk's glasses are in that bag." I reach in and grab them. The bag's empty beside his second helmet and two pairs of these things. We put everything in the hotel room.

Jett's watching me to see if I'm going to start this beast up right, and so when the engine roars to life, I hold his eyes as a challenge.

"Good enough for you?"

Under his breath, he growls, "Bitch."

"That's right. I'm a bitch."

"Forgot to tell you one thing," he smirks. "Actually, two."

"What?"

"Neutral is in between the gears, a half pull up on the pedal. Try it."

I test it and nod as the bike's gear sets. I can feel the difference. It's not pulling at me like a wild stallion waiting for the fence to be raised.

"What's the second thing?"

"Bitches are the best in bed." He grins and revs his engine.

"I hate you," I call over the rumble, but I'm stifling a smile.

"I hate you, too, baby. Now go."

Holy hell. I mean WOW. Why I've never done this before today, I'll never know. As the engine gets louder I shift up. The hog settles into a quiet roar until it's time to do that again.

Jett calls over the rumble, riding by my side, "Since no one's out here, slow down then stop!"

"Right here?"

He nods. We're in the middle of a two-lane road, but this town's population and that it's a desert, means it could be an hour before anyone drives up.

I slow the bike and shift down, concentrating on gripping and releasing the clutch beforehand, every time. As my boots hit the pavement, Jett smiles. "You're made for this, baby. Let's do it a few more times, then we'll take off."

"Okay," I nod, gripping tightly. When we're both satisfied I'm ready – and I mean really ready, not just so furious I think I'm omnipotent – we pull out and ride side by side to I-10 East.

Miles blur under my wheels and my hair blows behind me into knots but I couldn't care less about that.

This feeling is as close to flying as I've ever experienced. All the fear and anger I felt, sheds.

I start laughing like a crazy person.

Jett howls next to me, lets out a whoop and starts laughing, too. "It's a hell of a high, ain't it?!" he shouts over the wind.

"YES!"

After a few amazing moments, I cry out a sound of pure freedom. Without missing a beat, Jett joins in.

I've never felt so alive.

Matias is gone.

The whole world is open to me now.

I've been released.

No more vengeance.

It's over.

I am free.

LUNA

The trip on the way to South Vacherie was very light and fun for me. I let it be what it was because I wanted to savor the moments while I had them.

Jett and I stopped for food in San Antonio at Rosario's, a Mexican restaurant on a quaint Texas corner.

Because of the ride, the vibe was light and easy. We stuck to casual conversation. He asked if I ever got to the movies, I told him that I rarely did. He was the same.

He told me about the Ciphers and how they found him, his manner laid back as he explained, "I was a boxer. Yeah. It was fun. But you have managers. They book you fights. They tell you where to go, what to do. That's not my style. And I wasn't about to book the fights myself – felt uninteresting to me. A waste of my time."

He scooped salsa with a tortilla chip and chewed for a second, then continued.

"One night I was comin' home from a fight — my last fight, though I didn't know it at the time. I'd won. Feelin' good. And I heard this sound that rocked me. A woman was being attacked after the game. Two guys."

At my expression, he nodded.

"Yeah. Brutal. I heard the struggle before I saw anything, but when you hear something like that, you know what it is."

He smiled as if something good was coming, and leaned forward.

"Then I heard this fuckin' commotion like you wouldn't believe. Sounded like an explosion of fists and broken jaws. I was already runnin' over to help and when I turned the corner to the alley, there were the Ciphers kickin' the shit out of these two drunk guys. The girl was on the floor, staring at the chaos, stunned."

Jett did an impression of her face, making his eyes really big like he's seeing Godzilla looming above our table.

"I saw the Ciphers had the guys handled so I ran to the woman and helped her cover herself. She wrapped her arms around me and started cryin' while I told her it was gonna be alright."

"Where was this, Jett?" I asked him.

"Atlanta. Where my family is." He leaned back and stared off for a minute, maybe picturing them. Grabbing another chip, he grinned.

"I asked the Ciphers what their deal was. They told me. I've never looked back."

We stayed the night in Schulenburg, Texas because Jett said he prefers smaller towns. "Nicer people."

He got us two rooms at the Best Western Plus, Schulenburg Inn & Suites. It was nice, but the Maverick was cooler. The new place was more cold and professional. More for business people I guess? Which is not me or Jett, not at all.

As we went to our floor, with two separate keys in our hands, Jett said, "Goodnight, Sunshine."

I got the message his body language sent. He wasn't going to try to stay in my room, and I shouldn't try to stay in his.

This was the beginning of the end. Jett was putting distance between his heart and mine. I felt it in how casually friendly he was at dinner, and how little he touched me. It was like he was my brother or something...not that I'd ever had one. But he did. And I bet he treated them like that.

I couldn't sleep for a long time in that place last night. Couldn't stop my head from racing around the loss I was about to feel. Hell, I was feeling it already, just in the difference in how he was treating me.

I must have stared out the window at the stars for more than two hours.

He'll be your friend, Luna.

If you need him, he's the type of man you can call on.

Take comfort in that.

It's better than you've ever had.

Those words helped me close my eyes finally.

We're riding now, and miraculously the same feeling of freedom is in my veins. This rush is a temporary elixir to any kind of pain. It calms my soul, and looking over at Jett, I know he's just given me another gift. I needed this.

South Vacherie, Louisiana, what kind of a place are you? Why'd they pick you?

As we turn off the road onto a winding, oak tree lined driveway, Jett leads the way. A white plantation comes into view through the fog, one reminiscent of Tara in Gone With The Wind.

My questions are answered. It's beautiful, even with the need for paint. It looks like they left it looking a little haunted on purpose to honor the South's past.

Our engines rumble to a stop and through the fog-refracted lights on the porch I see the Tasmanian Devil called Honey Badger swing open the front door and whistle through his fingers, before shouting, "'BOUT TIME!!!"

Between majestic columns, he runs out and jogs down the steps to grab Jett as soon as he dismounts the bike. They give each other a big man-hug, smacking each other backs with grins on their faces.

"Been too long, buddy," Jett says with feeling.

I don't know which one's which of the other two guys who were at the motel that day I met Jett, but they appear next, with women who smile from the porch eyeing me.

Honey Badger's name is too hard to forget with the stories Jett told me about what happened, and how he protected me from jail, I have a genuine smile for him when he walks over to greet me.

"Lookin' better, girl! You were a fuckin' mess last time I saw you."

Laughing I nod, and he shakes my hand.

"I'm Scratch," the salt & pepper haired man says, walking with his hand out, too.

"Hey, what about me?" Jett calls to his back.

"I gotta see this miracle girl for myself," he calls out with fake anger. The frown disappears in a big smile as he shakes my hand. "We thought you were dead for sure."

"So I've heard," I smile, glancing to Jett. "Nice to meet you, Scratch."

"Fuse," the one who with a snaggle tooth says, shaking his head, just as surprised as the others to see me upright. "How was the ride?"

"Fucking incredible," I admit.

"I bet!" He turns to Jett. "How'd you get Tonk to agree to THAT?!!"

Jett crosses his arms and grins. "It was his idea."

"Fuckin' liar," Fuse mutters, turning to point to the enormous house. "That's my old lady, Melodi." The blonde woman gives a little wave. She's mid-thirties and from the look on her face, hard to crack. Fuse turns to me and says under his breath, "She'll warm up to you in time."

My lips part, but I stop myself from correcting him. It doesn't feel right to dampen the happy reunion with the news I'm not staying.

A black man with the same leather and patches

they all have, strolls out wiping his hands. "Jett! Fuck, it's been a long time, buddy."

"You cookin'?" Jett asks as he embraces the man.

"Jambalaya. You ready to have your stomach burned out?"

Jett laughs. "Hell yes. This is Luna."

The man turns to me with his hand out. I find it interesting that none of them are hugging me. I have a feeling it's an unspoken code among them: don't touch Ciphers' women. The politeness of the handshakes makes me suspect that is what's going on.

"Nice to meet you..." I trail off so he can fill in his name.

"Throb," he says with complete seriousness. All the men crack up. He breaks into a grin, dark skin pierced by brilliantly white, straight teeth. And boy, he's got a mouthful of them. "Nah, I'm kiddin' ya. I'm Scythe." He steps back to check out Tonk's Harley. "How's a little girl like you handle this ride."

"You're only calling me little because you're a giant," I dryly throw back.

Jett tells them all, and pretty loudly, "She handled that thing like she was born to ride. No more backseat for you, Sunshine." Then he lowers his voice with a wicked smile. "We told Tonk she knew how, but...she didn't."

They all start shaking their heads, grinning like

that's the worst thing we could have done. Even the women on the porch smile. A little boy runs out and flies down the steps. He jumps at Jett and is caught midair, brought into a hug. "Hey fucker! How ya been?"

Melodi calls down, "Jett Cocker, don't you swear like that at my Tyler, you sonofabitch!"

"Why were you gone so long?" Tyler asks Jett as he gets set back onto the asphalt.

"This was a lot longer than normal, huh Tay?" The little boy nods and Jett musses up his hair, jerking his chin toward the house and locking eyes with me. "Hungry?"

Everyone heads in, the bikes left behind. I glance back to Tonk's hog, thinking of what Jett said about my needing one. This feeling in my chest says he's right.

JETT

"She stickin' to it?" Scratch asks me as we walk out after dinner to put the Harleys away. We're not worried about theft. No one around would dare fuck with us. But wear and tear from weather isn't necessary when you've got a garage like ours.

"Yeah," I mutter, the smile I've been faking, gone now that she's not around. "Can't tame a feral animal, Scratch. You just get cut."

Over the dull sound of rolling wheels as we walk the bikes around the side of the plantation, I can hear Melodi, Hannah and Mona chatting in the sitting room upstairs. Scratch looks up to their silhouettes through the gauzy curtains, too. He chuckles.

"What?" I ask him.

"She sure doesn't fit in with them." He shoots me a look to see if I agree.

"She wouldn't stay here," I argue, irritated.

"What dya mean?"

"If she stayed with me, she'd be with me. She's one of us. She would hold her weight out there on the road."

He frowns, the idea of a woman-Cipher foreign. We put the bikes next to the others and he still hasn't said a word about my belief. But I don't give a crap what he thinks. I know Sunshine. I know I'm right.

But it doesn't matter.

She's leaving in the morning.

"Your mother called."

I step back like I've been hit. "What? Who is it? Who's hurt?!"

He grabs my arm. "No, nothin' like that. She wanted me to make you come to the wedding."

Relieved, I chuckle and rub my jaw. "Does she think I'm still six? What the fuck, Ma?"

"Melodi talked to her since I was out. Nancy told her your dad doesn't want you there—"

"—No shock there."

"—but your family does. She thinks I have more pull over you than she does now."

This hits me hard. "I'll call her."

"It's two weeks away."

"I know! I know. I know when my own brother's wedding is. I'll go. My mind's been occupied."

The truth is it's a good thing. This couldn't have come at a better time. I need to see them as much as they need to see me. It's been too long and gettin' over Sunshine is gonna be a fuckin' bitch. Jaxson and I need to have some beers. I want to thank Justin in person for helping us find Matias. Can't wait to tell him about Carmen and Tonk. Tell him he's a matchmaker. Jason can razz him for days over that one, because Justin is anything but romantic.

And Jake...gotta see him on the most important day of his life.

Just wish Jeremy could be there, too.

Scratch is about to close the garage. It's a manual door from the olden days, the kind with a padlock, so he's pulling on it, his eyes miles away. He always looks like that when we're here. He's our V.P. He gets the calls. He runs this house. Our President is in Montana – stays there most of the time now that he's old. I don't think twice about it. I'm just waitin.' So when Scratch throws the door back up and strolls into the garage with purpose, I just think he forgot somethin' inside.

"Jett, what the fuck you doin' out there? Get in here. I got something for you to see."

Uncrossing my arms I walk over to where he lifts a

tarp off a 1966 Triumph Bonneville T120R. Whistling at it, I nod. "That's a nice ride."

"Yeah, bought it for Laura." He gravely meets my eyes. "She never saw it. Fuckin' bitch." He turns back to gaze at the bike. "It's too small for the men. Why don't you give it to Sunshine?"

I blink in shock. "Scratch..."

"It's just sittin' here. What's that girl got? Nothin.' You say she can ride? Let her."

"So she can ride right out of here," I mutter on a long exhale.

We stare at it. He waits for me to think a minute before he side-eyeballs me. "Set it free."

"Yeah...but it's not comin' back to me. Kinda hard to let go when you know that."

"Don't I know it," he says on a long exhale.

Upstairs I search for Luna but can't find her.

"That girl's stuck up," Melodi tells me from her doorway.

"She's just quiet, Mel. You're the one who's stuck up."

"Thanks a lot!"

"Call 'em as I see 'em." I continue the search until I

find Luna in the backyard staring out at fog so thick you can't see when the lawn ends. "Hey."

Luna whispers, "I love the moss on the oak trees."

Walking up to her, I take in the view. "We get a lot of water here."

"How long has this property belonged to your club?"

"Way back. And during the days of slavery, the owner worked with the old Underground Railroad." Off Luna's curious look, I explain, "They smuggled slaves to the North for their freedom."

"Wow," she breathes. "Brave!"

"A lot of people died."

"I'm sure."

I can't believe I have to say goodbye to her in the morning. I'm still deep down hoping she changes her mind.

"I've got something to show you."

Luna looks at me from the corners of her beautiful eyes. "What?"

I just smile and start walking. The sound of her boots in the grass follows soon after. I told Scratch to leave the garage unlocked.

Upon sight of all the Harleys lined up with style, Luna sharply breathes in.

"Amazing, right?" I tap my baby as I pass her for the Triumph.

Luna follows me and slows down to take in the white and black classic. "Wow," she whispers, running her fingers over the smooth seat.

"It's yours."

Her hand freezes. "What?" She looks at me with a look I don't understand.

At least, not yet.

"Jett, I said I can't stay..."

"How are you going to leave? On foot?"

Fuck, it hurt to say that. Inhaling I stare back at her as she tries to understand what I'm tellin' her.

"You're giving me this not as a bribe but as a gift?"

Oh fuckin' hell.

That's what that look was.

Pissed off, I growl, "I don't need to bribe women, Sunshine. You got that?" Turning on my heels I head out.

"Jett!" she shouts at my back.

Throwing my hand in the air I flip her off.

"JETT!" She runs up and grabs my arm. "Stop! STOP IT!"

Tugging her off me I jab my finger in the air. "You don't want to be with me? I get it. You don't have to treat me like fuckin' dogshit. Jesus, woman! I'm a pretty smart motherfucker. I got the message. Did I fuckin' touch you last night? NO. I STAYED IN MY ROOM. I invite you into my home, give you one of the coolest rides on the road so you don't have to hitch, and what do you do? You stab me in my heart one last time. I'm done. I'm fuckin' done. Why don't you leave now!"

Her deep brown beauties fill up and she covers her mouth with her hands.

I feel eyes on us and cut a glance upstairs to find the women watchin' us from the window.

"THIS AIN'T A FUCKIN' SHOW!"

The curtains fly shut.

Digging into my jeans for the keys, I throw them to Luna. "It runs well. New tires. Scratch has O.C.D. when it comes to bikes. Gassed up and everything."

"Jett, I..." She shakes her head and runs her hands through her hair, rubbing the shaved part a little longer like she's remembering what I've done.

I wish I'd never met her.

"Bye Sunshine. Take care."

I'm standing at one of the front windows, bracing myself with my hand on the windowpane as I stare out through the gauze. I don't want to chance her catchin' me watchin' like this.

It's some time before I see her. While I wait I picture her unloading her things from Tonk's bike and transferring them to the Triumph. Was she cryin' when she did it?

There's the sound of that sweet engine.

Any second and she'll be drivin' off.

Fuck. This. Shit.

There she is.

I didn't tell her she could take my extra helmet, but there she goes riding off with it, her hair braided like she learned to do before we hit San Antonio. The knots were somethin' else, even though she said she didn't care.

The bike suits her size. None of us guys would have wanted it. Scratch earned my respect with this move.

Again.

I guess I owe him.

Heavy boots walk up behind me and I glance over as Honey Badger hits my back, trying to lend me comfort. "Sorry, man."

"Scratch..." I choke, unable to finish my sentence.

Honey says, "He told me what he did," his voice low and somber.

We watch the taillight disappear into the fog.

The lump in my throat grows edges.

I just shake my head real slow like.

"Fuuuuhhhhck this."

LUNA

I am a shell of myself.

Lost.

No.

Worse.

I have nowhere to go.

The wind on my face was nothing like how I felt when he was by my side.

I am empty.

Numb.

Scared.

Is this what I have to look forward to?

A life where I hurt myself because of my past?

Do I deserve love?

I don't know.

Those women at the Cipher's home base were

foreign to me. They were so confident in their men. Talking about private things.

"Fuse always bitches about how I'm crazy but when he comes back after a long ride, he's always got tears in his eyes before he kisses me hello." Melodi shared so openly. I think she was claiming him in front of me, but she had nothing to worry about. I could have told her that, if I'd found my voice. "They act all macho but they're just little boys who want to be loved underneath," she laughed.

While they all shared similar secrets, I stayed quiet. She hated that. I could tell she wanted the dirt on Jett, but what was my right? I couldn't say how good he was to me. I couldn't talk about him when I knew I was throwing away the only thing that had ever calmed my bones.

"What, you too good for us or somethin'?"

The other two women stared waiting for me to answer Melodi.

"No."

"Big talker," she muttered.

I got up and went out to the yard. As I passed by the kitchen, the guys were inside drinking beer and chowing down on even more of that delicious Jambalaya. Honey Badger was roaring about some shit they pulled in Tennessee while the other guys soaked it up. They paused as they heard the back screen door clang shut. Honey Badger poked his head out. "You okay, Luna?"

Hearing my real name surprised me. I guess Jett must have told him it. I couldn't remember if someone said it when I was introduced. My mind was as thick as the outside fog, with anxiety. "I'm fine. Just need some air."

With a knowing look, he rolled his eyes toward upstairs. "They're just sniffin' you out. Give it time."

I nodded, unable to tell him I wasn't staying past this night.

Especially since, as I looked out over the beautiful property, the spicy taste of dinner still in my mouth, I wanted to stay. I wanted it very badly. I wanted those women to like me. The Cipher men, too. I wanted this life. I wanted this family. I'd never had anything like this.

And I wanted Jett. I wanted to tell him I love him.

I love him deeply.

I was thinking up how to tell him I wanted to stay when he joined me outside. The familiar scent of him as he stood next to me lit my body up. The idea that we could start a life together was so intoxicating that I felt dizzy.

And then he gave me the bike and my old shit came up. I've had so many men try to give me things, with bad intentions.

I knew Jett wasn't like that.

But old habits don't go away just because you wish they would. I guess you have to work for that.

Watching him lose his mind, so hurt by my mistake, was terrible.

I didn't have to be psychic to know that being without him would haunt me forever.

"More coffee?"

I blink back to present time and look up at the diner waitress who's gotta be in her early sixties, but her hair and makeup are so done up she reminds me of Dolly Parton.

"What?"

"Coffee? Want some more?"

"Oh." I push the cup toward her. "Yeah, thanks. Didn't sleep well last night."

"Oh, I hate that! Well, let's fix you right up." As she pours it I stare at the emptiness in the booth opposite me, seeing Jett sliding in and calling that waitress Alice just to make me smile.

"I see a lot of sad faces in here, but yours is the worst," she mutters, setting the cup down.

Blinking back to her, I don't say anything.

She sighs and glances around the empty tables, then she takes a seat. "What's wrong, Sugar?"

"Sugar? Really?" I mutter. "Nothing. I'm good."

"If you're good then I'm the First Lady." She taps

hot pink nails on the table. "It's gotta be a man. He cheat on you?"

"Nope." My voice is dead. "And I don't think he ever would."

"So, it is a man that's got your face all frowny."

"I really don't feel like talking. I'm not the type." I pick up the coffee, smell it, then set it back down as she watches.

"You know what my nana used to say to me? She said, *God speaks to us from everywhere and everyone.* And I have to tell you, Sugar, the second I saw you sit down I thought what you needed was a mother."

My eyes dart up to her face.

This woman just stabbed me with a knife I didn't know she had.

Understanding she hit the spot, she nods, "I'm right, aren't I?" With kindness in her crinkles, she leans over and puts her cold hand on mine. "Did she die?"

For some reason I don't pull away. "Yeah."

"How long ago?"

"I was ten," I whisper, unable to look away even with my vision getting blurry.

"Oh honey, that's too young!" She squeezes my hand really softly.

She's wrecking me. And I can't do anything about it.

"Just pretend I'm her," she tells me.

"That's crazy," I mutter, trying to tug my hand back. She won't let me. Her grip isn't strong. It's rooted in persistent kindness. "My mother wasn't great at making decisions," I confess before I know what I'm doing.

She takes a deep breath and nods once. "Well, talk to me like she was."

"You're not going to let me out of this are you?"

A sad smile appears. "No."

On an awkward laugh, I shrug and squeeze her hand back. "You have to let this go. I'm not used to the whole touching thing."

"No."

"Jesus," I mutter.

"Go ahead, Sugar."

What do I have to lose?

"I used to know what I wanted to do with my life."

"Which is what? What did you want to do?"

"Something you wouldn't understand. But I did it. And now I don't have a purpose anymore. I'm just... wandering. I've been traveling for eight days on my own and it didn't have to be like this."

"Why? You married? Did you run away?"

"No," I whisper. "Not married. Just met someone who made my life...better." My voice is so filled with regret and emotion that it's only a low rasp now. "I broke his heart."

The bell dings and she lets go of my hand out of instinct, a slave to the sound. A couple is walking into the diner, chatting about something. On a quick frown, she taps the table with her nails and whispers, "Hold that thought."

As if I can think of anything else.

But she never comes back. The place starts filling up, and I scan for a wall clock to see why it suddenly got busy in here. Sure enough, there's one over the register telling me it's noon.

This must be how people feel in therapy sessions when their time is up.

Drinking down my coffee, I pull out Jett's card and lay it down. My plan is to pay him back when I can get some cash. I'll steal some soon. Not worried about that. There's always some asshole in a bar who will try to make an unwanted move. Then he gets his nuts kicked in, my knee to his face as he bends over, and his wallet stolen before he can even grunt, "Fucking bitch."

But Jett's going to think I'm an even bigger bitch when he sees these charges.

Still...he hasn't stopped the card. Huh...I hadn't thought about that.

Aloud, I whisper a question I'd never thought to ask, "Is he tracking me?" The idea that Jett might be nearby, making sure I'm okay, or trying to think of a way to talk to me immediately kicks my heart into gear.

The waitress hurries over. She's the only one on this shift. "I'm so sorry, Sugar! What horrible timin'!"

I hand over the card. "You helped."

"Oh good!" She takes it and returns quickly for me to sign, too busy to notice a man's name is on it:

Jerald Cocker.

Pretty sure I don't look like a Jerald. And neither, in fact, does Jett.

No wonder he's pissed at his dad.

Smiling at this thought, I wave to her. I'm almost out the door, the bell's still dinging, when she touches my back. "Sugar, when you said you broke his heart. Do you know you broke yours, too?"

As the cooks call, "ORDER UP!" she hurries away.

JETT

"Fuck, this is beautiful, man," I tell my brother Jaxson, as we sit over coffee in his renovated barn-house home, a toasty fire burning across from us. "This all reclaimed wood?"

He nods and points to the high ceiling. "Had all this redone. The frame is the barn that stood here, but the roof was useless. Those joists and beams there? I got those off an old church in southern Georgia. Preserved well because the townspeople cared for it more than their own homes back in the day. Place was being demolished, so I took the wood. Also the shutters you saw outside."

"You do all this yourself?"

"Hired guys, but I was in there workin' with them. You know me."

"I was gonna say," I smirk, intimating that my older brother would never let another man do his job.

He smiles, staring out eight feet high windows onto the farm he owns, dark green eyes filled with memories. "Pretty much every day they'd come back expectin' yesterday's job finished by me while they were home eatin' dinner."

I chuckle, because I can see him doing that. "I bet. Did they slack off?"

"Nah. Made 'em work harder. They didn't like me showin' 'em up. Got the job finished a few weeks earlier."

"Fuck," I chuckle, "That never happens."

"With incentive, it does. Ego inspires."

"That it does." I set my cup down on his rustic coffee table that's got a manly and solid iron foundation, and walk to the fireplace to throw another log on. "I could live here."

"Why don't you?"

Throwing him a look over my shoulder, I grab a poker and break up the charred wood. "You know what I do."

"I only asked because I knew you'd say that."

Laughing loudly, I toss a new log on and walk to stare at the view. It's a foggy morning, just like back in Louisiana, and of course that makes me think of her.

"I met a woman, Jax."

"No shit?"

On a long exhale, I mutter, "Yeah. Didn't work out though."

"She didn't like you gone most of the year?"

Huffing through my nose, I shake my head, only seeing Luna's face. "She's a loner." At his low laugh, I spin around and point at him. "Don't say it!"

"Taste o' your own medicine?"

"You fuckin' said it." I grumble. "And you should know, buddy."

He shrugs and kicks his boots onto the coffee table, making sure not to knock over my cup as he takes a sip from his own. I love his style, not just in how he restored this old barn with the combination of rock, metal and reclaimed gray and brown wood, but also in his dishes. Those mugs have big handles meant for a man's hand. You feel good drinking from them.

"I know I'm a loner, Jett. You know you are, too. That's why it's funny to me that you're heartbroken over a woman who's just like you. Not funny, but...you know what I mean."

"Yeah," I mutter, walking to one of the beams and leaning on it. "But those women on the road didn't know me long enough to love me. They just loved the idea. And the sex."

"They sure do get hung up on the sex, don't they?" he mutters from personal experience.

"I don't think enough men give it to them the way they want it."

"Yeah," he smirks. "Also women want what they can't have. If they think you can't be tamed, damn if they don't want to lasso and tie you upside down with a brand on your butt."

"Except the one you wish would do that." We stare at each other.

"How long you know her?"

"That's a complicated question. Gonna take a while to answer it."

"I've got all the time in the world," he says with patience.

Even though it's only six in the morning I ask, "Got any bourbon?"

"Just talk."

"Fuck," I mutter, and launch into it. Jaxson listens intently, asking questions when he needs clarity, and dropping his feet on the ground to lean forward and soak it all in. I tell him everything. No detail is spared. I make sure to tell him all the good things about her, and the bad. I've been dying to get this off my chest. It feels like I'm dead inside. I needed Jax.

Known him my whole life, which sounds weird, but he was there when I was born. The others came after. We had some time alone.

The twins were a unit beneath us in age, so Jaxson

and I have a closer bond than with the others. Growing up we were their leaders, but now that our brothers are all grown, I'd say none of them follow us in any way anymore. They're all their own men.

Jaxson's quieter than I am. He has a wise soul. Never asks anyone for anything. He's out here on this farm all by himself and likes it that way.

I've got my club and we rarely stay in one place for long.

So while we're both strong, we're different.

But we get each other.

He understands that when I say Luna is the one for me, I mean it.

"What're you gonna do, Jett? Made any decisions?"

"Yeah."

"What?"

"Nothin.' I'm doin' nothin.' She's got my card and is charging up hotels and food, but I'm leavin' it alone. She's got no one. She'll find her way. Get a job or steal the money. Hell, I don't know. Probably steal it, I guess. I can't see her workin' under some boss. The only consolation I have is I know she'd never sell herself in any way. Hell, after what she's been through? She's only been with three guys. I'm the third."

"No shit? Man, I have no idea how many women I've had."

"Me neither."

"It makes sense with her childhood. How old is she?"

"I never asked. Late twenties, I think. Looks like Penelope Cruz and acts like a Lynx in a cage after the sedatives wore off. And when she looks at me I want to eat her alive. I love her. I fuckin' love this bitch."

Jaxson nods, looking somber. "I'm sorry, man."

"Just gonna have to live without her. I was doin' that before we met." Turning back to look at the farm, I mutter to myself, "Just feels different now."

He lets me sit in it for a minute, but won't let me wallow. Changing the subject, Jaxson says, "I told mom you were on your way. Called her last night before you got here."

"You guys get tired of reportin' my whereabouts?"

His normally serious face breaks out into a slow grin. "With a family as big as ours, we always report on each other, Jett. You remember how it was before you went on the road..." He smiles at the memory. "...that one time when Jason was dating Becca in high school and she took his virginity. Shit—"

"—Jason told Justin first and then it was like three minutes before Mom hugged him and embarrassed the shit out of him by calling him a man!"

We're both laughing so hard now that Jaxson stutters, "Jeremy fuckin' shouldn't have told her! But oh man, that was funny!"

"So fuckin' funny! So good!"

"Jason's face!"

"I know! I'll never forget it!"

When the laughter dies down, Jaxson glances to the fireplace and stares at it for a while. "Wish Jeremy could be here for the wedding."

"He's in Syria again?"

"Yup. Just flew in. God better watch over him."

Over the crackling fire a hawk's distant cry sounds. As though it was an alarm for Jaxson, he stands and grabs up both cups, heading for the kitchen. He moves like a cowboy, real slow. Trustworthy. The layout is wide open so I can watch him over the stone island that houses four gas burners and a modern oven. In silence he pours more coffee while I turn back to the view and let the calm of the farm slip into my veins.

I wonder how my brother would do as a Cipher. The fighting would be different. He'd probably talk the fuckers we run up against, out of it, with his well-known powerful calm.

He'd never back down from a fight – I know that from experience. We've come up against some heat in the past. Atlanta knows the Cockers, and while most look up to us, they don't all like us. There's jealousy since our family's blood runs deep in this city, goes way back. And money has never been an issue, which pisses some off.

None of our ancestors squandered what they made – there were no gamblers among us, at least not when it came to money. They invested and saved and grew into an estate that would be passed down.

We're not the Rockefellers, but in an affordable place such as Atlanta, we've done well.

In some ways The Ciphers are like that, we live well but carefully. We don't squander. We save. Hell, that's one of Scratch's main gifts, making money grow and last so that we have a foundation. He and Mona handle the Louisiana branch. They're a team. Smart, together.

They're gonna have to teach one of us what they know.

Thinkin' on it, I'd be the perfect choice for them, with my history of caution. Overspending has never been my thing, thanks to my parents teaching me to respect the power of the dollar.

I guess that's one thing my dad did, more than my mom.

He always said, "If you don't need it, save the money for what you will need – or better yet, what you'll really want."

Great fuckin' advice.

As Jaxson ambles back over with a couple of full and steaming cups, he cocks an eyebrow at me. "What's with the smile?"

"I missed ya, Jax."

With a thoughtful gleam in his eyes Jaxson says, "Missed you, too. This woman...what's her name?"

"Sunshine," I answer without even thinking of calling her Luna. "Though I should have called her Storm."

He gives a low chuckle and takes a sip. "Wanna milk the cows with me? They're gonna be hurtin' if I wait much longer."

"Fuck yeah, I do!" I hit our cups together. "Teach me how."

As we head out, I cock an eyebrow at him. "Is this gonna make me think of her?"

Jaxson chuckles, "You're sick." After a second, he admits, "Probably."

LUNA

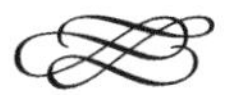

Oh my God, what is he going to say when he sees me? He asked me to go. Ordered me to leave, actually. He was so hurt and angry. Before then he'd been kind and as patient as possible, even under the crappy circumstances.

But I broke him down.

What's he going to say?

"Well, well well!" Melodi calls down from the front porch of the Cipher's plantation. "Never thought I'd see your stuck-up face again!"

Oh, fuck.

Taking off my helmet, I dismount the Triumph and eye her. "Jett home?"

Proud and protective, she shoots back, "What do you care?"

Hannah peeks out from the screen door. I see her whisper something, but it's too far away to hear what. Melodi frowns and mutters something back.

I hate knowing people are talking about me like this. Not a great feeling.

"Melodi, I think you have the wrong idea."

Snorting, she throws her hands on her hips. "I fuckin' doubt it."

"Luna?!!" I hear Carmen call from inside. She appears behind Hannah and pushes through. "LUNA!!!"

It didn't even dawn on me that Carmen and Tonk would be back by now. So good to see a friendly face.

"Carmen!"

We meet each other on the steps, hugging under Melodi's chafed glare.

"How was the train ride? How's Celia? How are you? All healed?" God, I didn't know how lonely I was until that tumbled out of me.

Nodding with a huge smile, she answers, "So fun! She's beautiful, come and see her! Tonk is on the road with the Ciphers. I'm almost healed. Feels a little funny if I touch it. Want to?" She motions to her dress. "I have to wear these because pants are too tight around where they cut me. Gonna be a big scar, too."

Even hyper-aware of our audience, I am still grinning at her. "It's so good to see you."

"Come and see Celia." She waves at Melodi. "Don't worry about her, she's the mother of the house. Real protective of everyone. And they all say you broke Jett's heart."

It feels like someone just slammed a sword in my chest. I glance to Melodi and Hannah as I walk past, feeling like the biggest piece of shit in the world.

"I don't like her being here," Melodi calls after Carmen.

Carmen patiently tells her, "She's my friend. She saved me, so I really don't care what you think! Sorry!"

Hannah blinks way too much from the discomfort of standing up to the matriarch. "You heard the story, Mel."

They both follow us inside to the old foyer. "Luna, you looked too surprised to see Carmen to be here for her."

I want to yell, *Fucking bitch,* but bite my tongue.

How dare she call me on that!

Especially because it's true!

"I already told you, Melodi, I'm here to see Jett."

"So you can play him like a fiddle again?" She crosses her arms.

Carmen whispers, "Let's just go."

"No. I don't run from fights. You want to do this, Melodi? You want a piece? Let's do it."

She glares at me through narrowing slits. "I would love to."

Hannah jumps between us. "NO NO NO!!"

We both look over as four children disappear from where they were spying on us. "Shit," Melodi mutters under her breath. She looks truly embarrassed, and human for once.

Hannah whispers hoarsely to her, "You promised them no more fighting."

"I know! Shit!" Shaking her head, she disappears after them.

Carmen and I exchange a look. We can't help but follow to find out what the hell that was all about.

In one of the downstairs bedrooms there are two beds. On one sits Melodi's son Tyler with tears in his eyes. She is kneeling in front of him. "I'm sorry, baby. You know Momma has a temper but I'm workin' on it. I'm not perfect, you know I'm not. But I'm tryin' to get better."

Sniffling, he whispers, "Uh huh!'

"I wasn't really going to hit her." She pauses. "Okay, maybe I was. But that wasn't the right thing to do, Love Bug! I was just really angry because of your uncle Jett."

"Okay," he sniffles.

She pulls him into her arms and sits on the bed,

glancing over to us. Whispering, she tells her only child, "Sometimes adults get angry just like you kids. Remember when you and Joanie were mad about the rabbit you found? When you both wanted it as a pet?" He nods a little as he rubs his eyes. "Remember how you pinched Joanie's arm so hard it left a mark? Well, that happens to us, too, baby. It's just a part of life. But I'm older than you so I should be able to control it better. I'm tryin', okay?"

"Uh huh!" His squeaky voice is so cute. I am just melted by this whole scene, and the defensiveness I felt with that woman isn't nearly as strong as it was.

I wish I could be a mother.

Melodi sets her son down and walks to me with a purpose. I step forward to meet her. She holds out her hand and says loud enough for him to hear. It's stilted but sincere. "I'm sorry I almost punched you. I was angry."

It's really hard for me not to smile right now. But I don't want her to think I'm laughing at her. I'm not at all doing that. This is taking some real guts – I can see it in her eyes how hard it is.

Carmen is standing in the doorway with Hannah and all three of hers and Scythe's children peeking through her legs.

We are on stage.

"It's okay, Melodi," I say in a louder voice, too. "I'm sorry I broke Uncle Jett's heart." Her eyes sharpen until I say with real honesty, "I couldn't admit I loved him. But I do. I love him very much."

Carmen lets out a sweet, ecstatic sound behind me.

JETT

"Holy shit!" I yell out as Jaxson and I stroll into the bar of Marcel, the dark, upscale, speak-easy-vibe restaurant in West Midtown, Atlanta. There's a sight for sore eyes. My three brothers who I haven't seen in way too fuckin' long shout a welcome and we all take turns hugging and smacking each other's backs.

"Jett, look at you!" Jason grins, "Man, it's good to see you. Jake, should get married more often."

Jake smirks, "Once is enough." He calls to the white-shirted, bearded bartender with a beer belly, "Tom! Finest bourbon for my brothers!"

"You got it, Jake," the guy nods, turning to the bottles.

"How was it staying at the ranch?" Justin asks me.

"Peaceful, man, peaceful."

Justin says to Jaxson, "I really need to come out there for a night or two. Get some fucking rest."

"Invite's always open," Jax smiles.

"Hey, Justin," I say, "I've been meaning to tell you — you did good."

"Yeah?"

"That's a first," his twin mutters. "What'd you do?"

"Nothing you wouldn't, if you had the power I have," Justin shoots back. To me, he asks, "All went well?"

"More than well," I tell him, while the others listen. The five of us together feels good. Only wish Jeremy was here to complete the circle. "The ring is done. Couldn't have done it without you." Keeping my voice low enough that we can't be overheard — not that anyone here cares about anyone other than themselves — I fill them all in with basic details of what we did. I guess if I had to admit it, I want them to know I'm not a piece of shit. That they can still look up to me.

Family is a strange thing, man. Their opinions matter more than anyone wishes they did.

Calm and serious, Jaxson reminds me, "Tell them about the baby."

"I was gettin' to it," I nod, leaning over to accept a

couple short rocks glasses from Tom. "Thanks man. Put it on Justin's bill."

"Asshole," Justin laughs, as Tom nods with amusement in his eyes and walks to the register.

Handing Jaxson his glass, I say, "One of my buddies – name is Tonk – he took to one of the girls. He's raising her baby as his own."

Jason whistles long and low. "That's fucking awesome."

"Yeah. We were there when she had the baby. Went into labor on the road."

The three raise their eyebrows and I tell them what happened. There's lots of laughing as I recount that it happened because Tonk and Carmen were going to have sex and things went in a whole different direction. Jake asks what they named her.

"Celia." Lots of nods of approval. "Looked like an alien, but they made it back to home base before I rode out here, and she's pretty cute now. You guys don't know Tonk, but this is a big deal for him. He's really steppin' up. We're all proud of him."

"Looks like the poor girl found a savior," Jake quietly says. "I didn't know stuff like that happened here."

"Happens everywhere," I tell him with gravity.

Jaxson's eyeing me. It didn't slip by him I kept Sunshine out of the story.

When I relayed everything to him yesterday morning, I didn't tell him the head of the trafficking ring was her father. I told him her mother was a victim, but not how far that went. And I told him Sunshine took him down, but that it was self-defense.

That's why the cops let her go, I explained, keeping details secret that only the people who went through it, should know.

But the reason I'm not talking about Luna here is I don't want to think about her. I don't want them thinking about anything but a happy ending, since it's Jake's bachelor party and this is a celebration.

I ask, to lighten things up, "We going to a strip club?"

Justin rolls his eyes. "Maybe you can talk him into one, Jett. He's fighting us."

Jake brings up his chin with a cocky smile. "Don't even try it. Won't work."

Jaxson chuckles under his breath. "I don't see Jake as the strip club type."

On a casual shrug, Jake says, "Why have hamburger when you've got steak?"

Mutual agreement all around.

"Speakin' of steak." I motion to the dining room. "Let's take this to a table. Starving."

As Justin pays the tab, the groom-to-be tells us how

Drew's been the opposite of the crazy bride, how she turned down Mom's wish for a big wedding, which is why we're having it at the house. "Her dad is marrying us."

"No shit?" I say with a smile. "Why?"

"He's a pastor. Guess I got his approval. Wasn't easy. They're old school so they weren't stoked about my being eight years younger than her. But they came around."

"Ready?" Justin throws his arm around me. "You had to wear the leather here, didn't you?"

Reaching to smack Jason, I say, "If this Hip Hop motherfucker can wear a hat inside a place like this, then I can wear my fuckin' patch."

"At least it's not my baseball hat," Jason laughs, touching his saggy, grey beanie.

"You look like a kid," I mutter as we all walk to the host stand. The pretty hostess stands straighter at the sight of five Cocker Brothers coming at her.

"I'll always be younger than you, Jett. Even when I'm seventy."

"Just think how stupid you'll look in that thing, then."

From the look on the hostess' face as she eyeballs Jason, he doesn't look stupid now. But I love to fuck with him. How he can listen to the crap he produces,

I'll never know. Mainstream has never been my thing. I hear he has a talent for it, but I wouldn't be the best judge. I'll just take Justin's word for it, since he knows Jason's work better.

LUNA

A dark-haired, brown-eyed woman in her late fifties answers the door. Since Jett is blonde and grey-eyed, I'm not sure who this is.

"Mrs. Cocker?"

"Yes?" Her eyebrows are up as her gaze drops to take me in.

I'm wearing my usual jeans and t-shirt with my black jacket. Boots, of course. And a small suitcase Melodi loaned me for the plane ride has replaced my backpack. But I feel very out of place at a home like this.

The residential neighborhood of Buckhead in Atlanta is very upscale and lovely. Huge lawns and even bigger homes. Lots of columns and brick. Birds chirping everywhere and I swear I just saw a fucking chipmunk.

"I'm Luna."

Her eyes light up. "Oh! I'm sorry! Is it two o'clock already? Come in!" She leads me into the large foyer and closes the door, glancing up to the sky first. "Still sunny. Let's hope that sticks for tomorrow!" Turning around, she glances at my outfit again.

"I uh…I'm not one for shopping. Just a basic type of girl, I guess."

She smiles, "Don't be silly. I was just takin' you in, honey, because between you and me, my Jett is a mystery to me lately. I'm just learning, is all."

"Ah," I whisper, glancing down to see what puzzle pieces she put together from me. "I guess we're a lot alike then. Not really fluffy."

She laughs and the sound is genuine. Ushering me further into the house, she leads the way. "When Melodi called me and told me about you, I have to admit, I jumped for joy. I hate to think of my sons being lonely and Jett…" she pauses, thinking of the words.

We walk into a kitchen that is so pretty I can't stop staring. A backyard the size of a small park is visible through the windows. Chairs are already set up for the ceremony. Tables, off to the side, wait to be dressed with cloth, flowers and food. It's the bare bones foundation of a celebration, and I can't believe I'm here, nervous as hell.

As she opens the refrigerator, I set my suitcase down by the wall so it's out of the way. I feel very much like I'm not supposed to be here, even with her being as kind as she is. This is just not my type of place. Way too homey, something I've never known.

Taking down a couple of glasses and pouring lemonade for us, she continues, "Jett has a wild side. Always has. Heck, I guess all my boys do, in their own ways. Boys are different than girls." She glances to me like I might be an exception. "Most of the time."

"Mrs. Cocker, I think it's very sweet of you to be helping me like this."

"Well, I'm doing it for Jett, honey," she smiles. "Ever since he went on the road with those men, I worry about him. I want him to be happy, and Melodi tells me that he loves you."

Hearing it said out loud like that makes my chest hurt. "She told you he's pretty mad at me." I'd listened to Melodi talk to Jett's mom for me, so I knew at least one side of the conversation.

Melodi and I discovered we're alike in some ways, both stubborn and strong.

We came to a mutual respect. Might even become friends. But who knows?

I don't mind a bitch as long as she's on my side.

"She did tell me that, yes. What happened, if I might ask? She didn't say."

Taking the cold glass from Jett's mother, I pause, staring at her. "Umm...I wasn't ready when he was. Your son's very..." I stop from saying, '*good,*' because then it sounds like I'm not good, and I don't want his mom knowing that. "...different, from the men I've met. I guess I needed some time to believe it."

And to think I might be worthy of being happy.

Another thing I'll keep to myself.

"He is that," she smiles with pride. "Let me show you your room."

"It was so nice of you to let me stay here, Mrs. Cocker." I had no idea why she offered that, until now. Manners are something she has in spades. She seems like the type of person who if she didn't like you, you'd never know it. She'd treat you with respect just the same.

Waving my gratitude away with her hand, she motions for me to bring my suitcase and follow her. "To tell you the truth, I was hoping you'd tell me a little about him!" Walking upstairs, she explains, "The hardest part of being a mother is when they grow up and move away. My Jeremy is in the Marines, did Jett tell you?"

"He did."

"I miss him like crazy. He had a ten-day leave after

boot camp before he had to go to that School of Infantry, then he got deployed and has been bouncing around ever since. Been a little over a year now. I was hoping he could come home for the wedding but he's needed there. It's this way, Luna." We pass photos of the brothers growing up – they line the long hallway's walls and my eyes zip over them as we pass, longing to linger.

Family.

What was it like growing up in a place like this?

I can't even wrap my head around it.

"We Skype all the time. I'm so happy for the Internet. How mothers of boys in the armed forces lived without it in days gone by, just makes me shudder to think of it. Must have been so lonely. It's right here." She opens a door to a good-sized room and surprises me by saying, "This was Jett's room growing up. I thought maybe you'd like to stay here."

Oh fuck. How my heart turned over when she said that.

Slowly walking in, I soak it all in.

There's a Led Zeppelin poster over an oak bed, a navy blue comforter pulled tight across it with matching pillows. On the dresser rests drumsticks, a book by Kurt Vonnegut and Hemingway, and boxing gloves.

As she says, "I cleaned out the clutter when he

moved out years ago, but kept what was most important. He's staying with Jaxson now. Hoped he'd stay with us, but..." she trails off, and I know from what Jett's told me that it's because of her husband that Jett's not here.

Picking up the dented drumsticks I turn them over in my hands. I wasn't sure where he was staying, and thought it might be here.

When I heard the quiet in the house I thought maybe the men were out somewhere. I've been waiting for him to walk in at any moment and give me a heart attack.

"He played drums?"

"He was terrible at them!" she says with a pained look. "Just awful. Banging away in here so we made him put them in the garage after one night of that! I can't even tell you how annoying it was. Don't tell him I said that, but good lord, you can't be good at everything!" She walks to the gloves. "This though, he was great at this. Hard for a mother to watch her son getting punched, but Jett gave more than he got. I only went to one match. Too much for me."

Smiling, I can imagine how weird that must have been for her. "I've seen his skill. He's very good."

Her eyebrows rise up. "Oh?"

Shit.

"They deserved it," I offer, knowing I just said something I shouldn't.

Mrs. Cocker crosses her arms. "Please tell me more than that." She's not upset, just wants to be on the inside. But I can't tell her what happened, because I don't want this nice woman, the mom of the man I love, to know where I come from. She already looks at me like I'm a foreign object and not one of her tribe. What would she think if she knew just how dark my past is?

"Please," she softly says.

Blinking to the carpet, I wring my hands. "Mrs. Cocker, umm, The Ciphers help people. That's really all I can say. It's their private business."

"I'm his mother!"

"I know." We stare at each other. "What do you want me to say, Mrs. Cocker?"

"The truth."

Sighing, I finally concede. "They kick people's ass and take bad people out of the picture."

Her eyes register this and with a somber steadiness she asks me, "Do they kill people?"

"No, they'd never do that."

Her shoulders slump with relief. "Oh, good. I was so worried." She glances away and I stare at her, thinking, *sometimes being a good liar isn't a bad thing.*

"Are you tired, Luna?"

"More nervous than anything."

"Anything I can do for you?"

There is one thing, but I don't feel right asking. "You've got a lot going on."

Her hands go up. "Are you kidding? Everything is ready! I can't put the linens on the table until tomorrow or the birds will dirty them. The flowers don't get here until the morning. The caterers are taking care of the food, also doesn't come 'til morning. My husband and the boys are all at the shooting range, for Pete's sake. Drew's mother is in town and isn't letting me help with her dress or anything. So infuriating. I'm just sitting here wishing I had something to do because I'm crawling out of my skin!"

Smiling at her exasperation, I offer, "Well, Melodi loaned me a dress, but now that I'm here, I realize it's a little too skimpy."

Mrs. Cocker blinks at me, then explodes...

"Oh THANK GOD! Let's go shopping!!"

JETT

From where I'm lying on Jaxson's couch, napping under the waning sunlight drifting in through the windows, I hear his phone ring, and him rise from where he was reading.

"Hey Mom, what's up?" He pauses a while then says under his breath, "No shit." There's a long silence that feels like it's something serious. Opening my eyes, I twist around to be able to see his expression. He's staring at me. "I think I have to tell him." Another silence.

"Tell me what?" Throwing bare feet onto his rug I rise up and go for the phone with my hand out. "Give me that."

He steps back and holds his hand out as a shield. "He'll want to know, Ma. Sorry." He hangs up.

"What the fuck! Who's hurt?"

"There's some girl named Luna at the house, Jett. Mom thinks you guys are together or something."

"Holy shit," I rasp, my eyes widening to dinner plates. "Fuck! No way!"

Spinning around, I start to pace, totally forgetting in my stupor that I told Jax her name was Sunshine, and he wouldn't know this is the same girl.

"Jesus, Jett, is this some chick you knocked up or something? She tracked you down?"

Frowning over my shoulder, I growl, "What? No! It's the girl! It's her!"

His head shakes like he's been punched. "You said her name was Sunshine!"

"I call her Sunshine. Because she's...fuck it. IT'S HER." Back to pacing, I snarl under my breath, "What the fuck is she doing at our parents' house? What'd Mom say?"

"Uh...I'm just wrapping my head around this. Let me think. She said the girl is here to be with you. They went shopping."

We stare at each other until I explode, "I'm napping on your fuckin' couch and Luna is shopping with my mom?!! WHAT THE FUCK?!"

Angry strides take me to the coat rack where I swipe my jacket down and struggle to get my arms in, missing the first time. "I can't believe it."

"Jett, put some shoes on."

"FUCK! Where'd I put 'em?"

He points to the end of the couch where they wait with the socks tucked inside.

Yanking them on has never been so hard. My hands are shaking. I have to try a couple times to shove my foot in. Off to my side I hear Jaxson grab his keys.

"I'm going with you. I have to meet her."

"Jax..." I growl.

He looks over from where he's putting on his brown, farming work-boots. We lock eyes. His eyebrows are raised, face somber. "I know. It'll be dinnertime when we get there."

"Yup." I head for the door. "How ya doin' Dad? Time to face your favorite boy."

With Jaxson's Jeep Wrangler following my Harley, we ride the hour back to Atlanta. He'd asked me before he climbed in if I wanted to call and warn them.

"No fuckin' way."

She didn't warn me she was comin.'

What the hell is this sneaky bitch up to?

At my parents' house?!

I'd noticed – oh, I noticed – that the credit

card transactions stopped a few days back. How'd she get the money to ride that bike here? Where'd she stay when she was on the road, and who with?

I roar into the warm wind, "WHAT'S SHE DOIN' AT MY FUCKIN' PARENTS' HOUSE?!"

I'm wound tight as the Harley rumbles up the multi-car driveway. Jaxson and I drive right on up. I jump off, unstrapping my helmet to throw it on the grass. My brother's footsteps are right behind me. We share a look.

"You ready?"

"Shit," he mutters, but nods. "Yup."

I raise my hand.

"You're knocking?" he asks under his breath.

Banging on the door with my fist, I wait. "Gotta be polite," I say on a wink filled with the devil.

The door opens wide and Dad is standing there.

Seeing him is like being punched in the gut.

From the look on his face, he didn't expect me. Ever.

He came to the door, protectively. Hearing the violent knock made him tell Mom, Luna and whoever else might be inside, to wait there while he checked it out.

He looks between us, trying to handle his own reaction at seeing his second son for the first time in four years. "Jerald. Jaxson." His eyes narrow. "Do you have to make a scene?"

"Guess so," I grate. "Good to see you, too, Dad."

His lips go tight and he exhales through his nose. Looking at this man is like looking in a mirror from the future. Me when I'm his age. I'm the one who looks the most like Congressman Michael Cocker, and I'm the least one like him.

I'd never wear those boring-ass fuckin' tan slacks and white button-up, for example.

And I wouldn't shun my own son for goin' his own way.

"Who is it, Michael?" I hear Mom ask from a distance, her delicate footsteps growing louder. She sees me and screams, "JETT!!!" and throws her arms open. Dad steps out of the way and I give Mom a big hug, locking eyes with him over her shoulder.

"Good to see you, Mom. You look good."

"Oh Jett, I didn't think I'd see you until...oh, you're here because of..." She pulls away and looks at Jaxson. "Why didn't you tell me you were coming?"

With a frank, coldness Dad answers for Jax. "Because I would have told them not to."

"That's right!" I grin with anger behind my eyes. "Can't say I went against your wishes because we didn't give you a chance to voice 'em! See that? Sneaky fucker, that's your boy!"

"Jett," Jaxson mutters to rein me in.

"Mom, I love you, and I will take you out for lunch before I leave town, but right now I'm here for Luna. Where the fuck is she?"

"I'm here, Jett," comes a voice behind my parents. It's surreal to hear that deep, sensual sound I've missed so fuckin' much, right here in the place where I grew up.

Mom steps back, warily eyeing me because she can see I'm in a real bad mood.

And there stands Sunshine, barefoot in a light blue summer dress, her hair brushed and clean, parted over the side with the shorter part concealed.

Her cheeks are flushed.

She looks absolutely beautiful.

I was going to yell at her.

I was going to yell at Dad.

But I can't even breathe.

Everyone is silent as she walks to me. "Jett," she whispers like she wants to touch me, but is afraid to.

"What are you doin' here?" I rasp.

"I'm so sorry," she whispers.

"We were just having dinner," Dad interrupts. The way he said it wasn't an invitation for me to join.

"I don't give a shit," I growl, turning to lock eyes with my father. "It's just food."

"Jerald, don't talk to me like that in my own home!"

"YOU MEAN HOW YOU TALK TO ME?!"

Holding back his temper, he grates, "I do not swear in front of women."

Luna whispers, "Mr. Cocker—"

Mom cuts her off. "—This isn't about us, Luna."

Dad's voice is high and mighty like he's talking from a podium. "Yes it is. It is improper and indecent to use that kind of ignorant, sub-human language when ladies are present."

Jaxson's deep voice rises in protest, "Dad! Come on!"

I'm so pissed I can't even see straight. "Did you just call me stupid?"

"Low class people use ignorant language and you weren't raised low class."

"Oh fuck," I snarl. "You are such a fuckin' hypocrite. Yes, I used the word again right there... twice!! What was it you said to me when you saw this?!!" I point at my Ciphers jacket. "You said – and I quote – Get out of my FUCKIN' HOUSE!"

"I never said that word."

"YES YOU DID!"

"NO, I DID NOT!" He gets in my face, the same height as I am. "But I will say it again, the way I said it the first time. GET OUT OF MY HOUSE."

"FUCKIN' HOUSE."

"JERALD!"

"It's JETT! MY NAME IS JETT!"

I feel feminine hands pull at me. It's a good thing Mom came in before I was about to punch him. I love the bastard, but I hate him. It would have been a bad day if we'd come to blows. I don't know how I would have recovered.

But it's not Mom.

It's Luna's voice I hear behind me. "Mr. Cocker, I'm sorry to have to say this after you've been so nice to me, but Jett is the best man I've ever met in my life, so you're being a fucking asshole right now."

Dad's eyes go really wide and Mom makes a small gasp off to my right. I turn to see Sunshine staring at my Dad with defiance and pride. Her beautiful brown eyes snap to me and she says, "Let's go, baby."

Since Jaxson has always had his head firmly on his shoulders, he remembers to ask Mom, "Does she have any of her things we need to take with us?"

"Yes. I'll be right back."

Sunshine offers, "I'll go with you, Mrs. Cocker."

"No, thank you. I'll be right back." Mom looks stunned as she heads for the stairs. I could tell she liked Luna before...but she doesn't know what to think now.

I'm sure she's torn by the disrespect that was just shown to her husband, who she loves very much and always will, to the loyalty just shown to her son.

I grab Luna's hand and turn to take her out of there, throwing a glowering look at my father.

From the staircase, Mom stops me. "Jett!"

Over my shoulder, I meet her eyes. "Yeah, Ma?"

"Please come to the wedding."

"He's no longer invited!"

"YES, HE IS," she shouts to Dad. "He is coming to Jake's wedding. He's his brother. He's your son. This is just awful!" Bursting into tears, Mom rushes upstairs, wishing our family was a better one.

Jaxson waits inside while I take Luna out to the front lawn. My fingers are strangling hers and I'm staring at the freshly cut grass. Looking over I meet her steady gaze and she touches my face. I nod once and close my eyes as she presses her warm palm into my skin.

Pulling her to me I hug her and kiss the top of her head. We separate as Jaxson comes out. Heading for his jeep, he says, "You can ride with me, Luna, since you're in a dress."

"Fuck that," she mutters, low enough that her voice doesn't travel.

Jaxson nods and hauls a small suitcase into the back, hanging up a garment bag on a hook inside by the backseat. "You guys staying with me?"

"That okay?" I ask him.

"Of course. I want you to be there." He holds my

eyes to let me know he's my brother and wants me around. Right now, that hits home in a way I can't describe. Thankfully, he'd never need me to try.

I climb on the Harley and exhale as Luna wraps her hand around my arm to help her rise up and throw her leg over. She hikes up her dress and presses up against my backside, tucking the fabric so that it stays modest. I clamp a hand on her bare knee before I start the engine.

I hear Mom call out, "Wait!"

She runs over with Luna's boots. "You left these in the bathroom. You can't ride a motorcycle in bare feet."

Jaxson helps put them on so we can leave as quickly as possible, while Mom stands by, staring at me like she's just crushed by all of this. Her arms are crossed and she's nervously fingering the pendant on her gold necklace.

Sunshine tells her, "Mrs. Cocker, thank you for being so wonderful to me."

"Just be wonderful to my son," my mom whispers back.

We take off.

JETT

"Thanks, Jax," I tell my brother as he brings Luna's things into his home.

"No problem."

"C'mon, Sunshine." Taking her hand I lead her out into the three-hundred-and-forty acres of farmland my brother bought when he got the loan right out of college.

She's silent. I'm the same, just looking forward to guide us to the trees up ahead. "Watch out for that," I mutter, stepping around a cow pie I almost didn't see because it's so dark out here now.

She steps around it. "Thanks."

My brain is still boiling with anger at my dad, at her, at not knowing what to say. Sometimes being a man sucks. Can't get your head straight when you're this pissed off. All I see is red.

Under the private canopy of White Oak trees, the moonlight is nearly stamped out. Our eyes are adjusted to the darkness now, and when I face her I can see she's biting her bottom lip. "I don't know where to start, Luna. I've got so many fuckin' questions."

"Jett," she rasps, full of emotion. "I'm so happy to see you."

Groaning, I pull her into my arms and look down into her beautiful, dark eyes. "You okay? Have you been alright?"

"No."

"Anybody hurt you?"

"Only me. I'm the one who hurts me."

I kiss her hard and she responds with the same urgent need to be close to me as I feel for her. Gasping away so I can get some answers, I search her face and demand, "What does this mean, baby? Where do you stand?"

She buries her face into my neck and kisses it, squeezing me in the strongest hug she can. Looking at me she says, "Can I please be with you?"

"For how long," I rasp.

"As long as you want."

"How long do YOU want?"

She blinks and shakes her head. "You're going to make me say it, aren't you?"

"Yeah. Say it."

Jeeezus, after what she put me through, I want her to scream it. I need to know that what I think is going on here, is really fuckin' happening, because I've got way too much hope for one man to feel.

"I love you, Jett."

Fuck.

This is why they call it heartache.

There is actual pain in my chest, hearing those words falling from those lips.

Husky and low, I whisper, "Say it again."

She slowly repeats, "I love you...I love you...I love you."

I kiss her like I've never kissed anyone. It's passionate and angry and relieved. She meets me every step of the way, tasting just as good as I remember. Lowering her to the grassy earth we both pull her dress up and yank my pants down.

No time for foreplay.

We need to be one.

Never stopping kissing her, I enter her body and meet her moan with a growl of aching need I've never felt. We move without thinking.

All instinct. Like cavemen who've never evolved.

We bite each other.

Claw at bare skin.

Rip clothing.

Fuck each other like someone's holding a gun to our heads, saying, *FASTER*.

There are no words between Sunshine and I as we fuck in the darkness on the cool grass.

No telling her what I'm gonna do.

She's not moaning my name.

Only *people* can talk.

We're something less than that right now.

Primal.

Shameless.

Unhinged.

When she screams and cums so hard that I see white-hot heat and explode into her pussy with every ounce of juicy heat I've got, it isn't enough. We do it again. And again.

When my cock finally passes out, Luna is lying on me, panting just as heavily as I am. I can see stars through the separation of trees. Millions of 'em. You never see these in the city. We have 'em in Louisiana, but tonight they're different.

Stroking her hair with exhausted fingers, I rasp, "I love you, Sunshine."

She burrows deeper into me. "I can't get close enough to you."

"I know the feelin.'"

"I took your credit card again, Jett."

A tired chuckle rumbles out of my chest. "No shit."

Tracing my ribcage, she asks, "You knew?"

"Yep. Noticed when you stopped using it, too. What happened? Get a job?"

Her turn to chuckle. "Not exactly the good worker, type."

"What, then?"

"Melodi gave me hers. You have to pay her back."

"No shit?" Same words, new meaning.

Luna rises up to look at me. "She and I kinda had it out, and now we might be – I'm not saying we will, but we MIGHT – be friends."

My eyebrows twitch on a smile. "You charmed the cobra?"

"More like almost beat the cobra up, and gained her respect," she smiles, kissing me. "She's sneaky, though. I like that. I told her I had your card and she said, *Oh, he's probably watching you, so we better give you a new card so he doesn't see you comin.*'"

"What the hell were you going to do, just show up at the wedding?"

Luna shrugs. "I didn't know exactly. I thought you might be at your parents' house, but now I know that wasn't really a possibility."

"Nope. Not at all." I close my eyes and enjoy the light caresses of her fingertips as she runs them all over my face, no part left untouched. "We'll get your bike out of the garage tomorrow."

"It's back in Louisiana."

"It is? How'd you get here?"

"Plane. After being on my own for so long, I wanted to ride with you, so I could feel you up."

Laughing, I kiss her. "You can feel me up all day and all night, for as long as you want, baby."

"For how long?" she asks, parroting me from earlier. I guess she needs me to say it. I can understand that, knowing her.

Gently grabbing a fistful of her hair, I lift my own head off the ground and come real close to her beautiful face. "You and me are forever, Sunshine. That's how long."

Feeling my cock twitch back to life against her thigh, she smiles. "Show me."

No fuckin' problem there.

LUNA

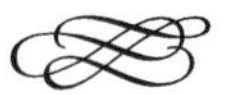

The fog over the farm in the morning light adds to the peace I'm feeling today. Jaxson and Jett are cooking up bacon and eggs for us while I sit on a stool, watching them, the view beautiful through the window behind them. Jett's got no shirt on, so of course I'm staring at his back. Jaxson has a Henley shirt on. They're both in jeans, Jett's darker than his brother's. Their family comes well made.

No one's speaking, and it's a comfortable silence. The two of them easily move around each other like only people raised together can, I guess. It's kind of like a dance, no one bumping into the other as they pull out plates, pour glasses of orange juice, butter toast, and grab silverware.

It's a different energy than at the plantation where the people are rowdy and children run free.

I wonder if Jaxson gets lonely.

He's out here all by himself.

Maybe he doesn't know it, even if he is.

I never knew I was. Not until I met Jett.

I thought I was fine.

I wasn't.

It hasn't sunk in that I have a partner on this ride now. But I'm willing to sit and wait for it to. I'm scared. But I *want* this.

"Let me bring those over," I say, walking over for the juice glasses.

"Jax, you got the—"

"—Yep," he answers before the question is finished, and reaches for salt and pepper.

Jett winks at me. "Sunshine likes her salt."

I can't help but grin. "Ah, he knows me."

"Gettin' there."

As we walk over to the grey and brown wood dining table– I think to myself, *ever since I met you you've known me, even better than I do.*

"Luna, how was it shopping with our Mom?" Jaxson asks before he digs in.

Thinking of the few hours she and I spent in Lenox mall, I answer, "Strange, but nice. She's a good person." Both brothers make grunts of agreement, both equally focused on food. I'm not sure if I should tell them this, but I try it anyway. "Your dad was good, too."

Two pairs of eyes shoot up to lock on me.

Picking up the saltshaker, I carefully explain, "He knew I was here for you, Jett. He asked about you."

"He did?" Jett drops his fork.

"It wasn't a lot of words or anything. When he got home last night from work, she introduced me and explained that you and I had a fight, but that you loved me."

Jaxson sips his coffee, side-eyeballing his brother.

Jett just inhales really deeply, waiting for more.

"They talked about his day while your mother made dinner. I just stood by with a glass of Sauvignon Blanc, which I'd never had before."

"Mom loved Sauvignon Blanc," Jett mumbles, still waiting for details about his dad.

She does. She had several.

But I leave that part out.

I might have made her nervous. I do that.

"Then when we sat down to eat, he just kinda casually threw it out there: *How is Jerald?*"

"Fuckin' hate that name."

"It was our grandfather's," Jaxson explains to me. "But it never fit Jett."

"No," I agree. "When he asked, I could tell it was

hard for him to, and harder for him not to, if that makes sense."

"Yeah," Jett mutters. "What'd you tell him?"

"I said that you're really happy with your life. That you're helping people."

"What'd he say to that?"

Glancing to my plate, I confess, "He rolled his eyes."

"Dick!"

"But I think it's more important that he asked."

We eat in silence for a while and I devour my food in no time, looking up to find both brothers watching me with amusement. "See what I told you?" Jett asks. "She eats like a man. Fuckin' love you, Sunshine."

Grinning with my mouth full, I proudly tell him, "I love you, too."

Jett whoops really loudly, which makes Jaxson start laughing. An alarm goes off on his phone. He lifts it up and says, "Time to get ready."

JETT

When Luna comes out of Jaxson's bathroom, my jaw drops. "Wow."

She glances down to the blue, floral print dress she and my mom bought for the wedding, and smiles with a shyness she's never had before now. "Yeah?"

"Yeah," I nod, walking to her. She lets me spin her around. "What is this?"

"Chiffon, I think? That's what she called it. I like that my huge tits aren't on display."

Laughing at her bluntness, I agree, "You look really elegant, baby. Lovely. No, fuck that, you're a stunner." Yelling to my brother as he walks in from checking on his ripening tomato garden, I warn him, "Don't look, Jaxson, she's all mine!"

He grins and grabs his coat. "You look great, Luna. But I'm more into you right now, Jett. Haven't seen you in a suit since Grandpa's funeral."

Spinning around I ask my woman, "Clean up pretty nice, don't I?"

She adjusts the strap on her heels and rises up to kiss me. "You're so fucking hot I can't even think."

Laughing, I pull her closer and kiss her deeper. "You go on without us, Jax."

"Nice try," he calls back. "Come on."

As I go, Luna slaps my ass, hard. I grab her hand and kiss her fingers before entwining them with mine.

We ride over in Jaxson's Jeep, talking easily about his farm. Luna declined milking the cows this morning, but she asks my brother a lot of questions and keeps him occupied. As we get closer I feel tension hit. Soon they both feel it and a quiet takes over the remainder of the ride. No one among us is the talk-when-you're-uncomfortable type.

The street is jammed with parked cars by the time we arrive. A valet station with four drivers running around is set right in front of the house. There are lavender and white flower petals all over the lawn, and the door is wide open as well-dressed people walk in, most of the faces familiar.

"Here goes nothin,'" I say as we all climb out.

While Jaxson gives his keys over to a valet, Luna tells me in a low voice, "If you want to leave early, we can."

I squeeze her hand and shake my head.

That ain't gonna happen.

I don't run away from anything.

And I'm invited here.

My dad doesn't matter today.

It's all about Jake.

I'm a member of this family, goddammit.

Inside is crowded with guests. People I haven't seen in years greet me. Aunt Anna and Uncle Dave, my cousins, and friends of the family we've known since we were born. Everyone's happy to see me, and the feeling is mutual. Luna says little as I introduce her over and over. She just smiles and accepts the handshakes and compliments. "She's so lovely!" we hear a lot.

At one point as some people walk away, I whisper in her ear, "Little do they know you could kick their asses."

She grins. "I so could."

Under it all is a feeling of unease as I look for my dad around every corner, not wanting to be surprised.

There he is.

He's outside.

Just saw him chatting with a big smile on his face, to a couple of people I don't remember the names of. I know they're friends of my parents' from church.

My brothers are out there, too. I want them to meet Luna before the ceremony starts. "Baby, come on outside."

"I'm here with you," she whispers, squeezing my hand, spotting my father, too.

"I'm good. It's all good."

As soon as we walk onto the wide back porch that leads to the lawn by way of a few stairs, Jason and Justin spot me. "JETT!" they yell out over the conversations, so loudly that most of the people look over. Michael Cocker, too. Dad and I lock eyes as my brothers make their way through the crowd. Jason's in a grey suit, Justin in navy blue.

"Come on, baby." I lead Luna down the stairs to meet them. They spot her, see us holding hands and at the confusion on their identical faces, I remember I'd never told them about her. "Guys, this is the love of my life."

"WHAT?!"

"SINCE WHEN?"

Luna blushes, staring back at them and realizing they have no idea who she is.

Justin, the bastard rakes an appreciative look over her and says, "Holy shit."

I smack his chest hard with my free hand. "Hey!"

Grabbing where I hit him, he laughs. "I couldn't help it. *What* is the deal here?"

"It's a long story," I grin. "Luna, this asshole is Justin. That's how you can tell them apart. He's the dick."

"Hey!"

"And this is Jason. He's—"

"Got terrible taste in music," she finishes for me.

Jason laughs loudly. "Oh oh!! I see how it is. Trained her, did you? Bet you didn't have her actually LISTEN to any of it."

"I didn't want to scare her off," I smirk. "Where's Jake?"

"With grandma." Justin points past the people.

"Can't see him from here. I'll head over. Want him to meet you," I tell Luna, leaning down to give her a kiss.

"What the hell, Jett, seriously," Jason says.

"Yeah, man. Were you joking, or..."

Luna answers for me. "He's joking. I just met him outside."

Choking back a laugh, I nod. "Yep."

They stare at us, not sure what to believe. But then Mom hurries over and ruins it.

"Luna! Oh, look how pretty that dress is. It's

perfect! The dressing room did it no justice. Out here it just shines!"

I steal a glance to Jason and Justin and they're glaring at me, the first with his hands in his pockets, the latter crossing his arms.

"Thank you, Mrs. Cocker. I'm sorry about last night."

Mom loses the smile for a moment, but being such a seasoned hostess, it comes back as quickly as it left. "It's an ongoing feud, honey. Nothing to do with you. I'm just happy you both came."

I let go of Luna and give Mom the hug she wants. "Sorry, Ma. Lost my temper."

"I know. You both always do that. You're just too alike is the problem, in all the wrong ways."

Justin asks, his voice weighted, "Run in with Dad?"

"Yeah. Probably won't be talking to him today."

"Oh!" Mom cries out, seeing kids eyeing the wedding cake like they're going to stick their fingers in it. She runs off to stop them.

"Let me introduce you to Jake, Sunshine."

"We want the story, Jett!" Jason calls out.

"Well, then don't just stand there with your panties in a bunch. Follow us!" I tell him, taking Luna's hand and leading her across the grass. We nod and smile to people as we make our way through.

Jake's kneeling in front of Grandma and since she's

pretty deaf, we overhear her loud voice telling him, "You just have to forgive each other. Talk things out, but not everything. Some things you just let go!" He's nodding, soaking it all in when he sees me coming. His eyes dart to my hand, and at how it's not empty, then cut to her face. He rises up with a frown, the same confusion they had.

"Giving him marriage advice, Grams?"

She looks over from her chair and explodes into surprise. "Jerald!!"

She's the only one who can call me that and I'll never mind. It's her husband I was named after. I miss the guy. He was good. A quiet man. Served in World War II. Sure did love our Grandma.

I give her a hug and lift her from her chair, then set her back down. "I'm gonna cuss up a storm, Grams. Just warnin' ya."

"Don't you dare!"

Reaching for Luna, I say, "I want to introduce you to my lady."

Luna with her dark beauty and that beautiful dress complementing her olive skin, steps up and gets the once over from my grandma...three times. "Hi, Mrs. Cocker."

"Well, aren't you a pretty thing?"

After he received only irritated shrugs from the twins, Jake is done being patient. "Jett..."

I turn to him. "Luna, this is the man who's getting married today. Jake, Luna. Luna, Jake."

He shakes her hand. "It's very nice to meet you."

"He does look like Nancy," Sunshine tells me, glancing to the brothers.

Justin and Jason have ice-green eyes and blonde hair like mine. Only they're more model-handsome. I'm more kick-the-shit-out-of-you.

Jake, he's darker skinned and brown-eyed, just like Ma.

"Jeremy looks more like Jake and Ma, too, baby."

Grandma demands, "Jett, did you get married without telling us?"

"Not yet, Gorgeous," I grin, grabbing her fragile hand and kissing it, with a wink. "But if we do, we'll probably elope. Luna and I aren't the big-wedding types." I look to her for agreement and she nods with a look that says, *no fuckin' way are we doing this shit.*

Jake crosses his arms as the twins walk over to stand on either side of him, like an interrogation is about to happen. Jaxson strolls over and sees this. "Surprised?"

The three of them look over and realize he already knows.

Just for the fun of it, Jax rubs it in. "They've been staying with me."

"WHAT?!"

My older brother and I start cracking up. "Shit, your faces!"

"Language!" Grandma cries out.

The three left outside the joke, stifle grins. Jake finally exhales. "Okay, come on. Enough is enough."

JETT

I tell them we met on the road a few months ago, and have been taking it slow. I glance to Jaxson to wordlessly let him know that he's the only one who'll get to know the real story.

Dad's voice interrupts me as he yells to the crowd, "Alright everyone, let's take our seats."

"I'm really happy for you, Jett," Jake tells me, shaking my hand with a look that says he never thought he'd see the day. Doesn't surprise me. When I saw him in Colorado I was banging some bartender I can't even remember the name of.

Now look at me.

Introducing her to my whole family, and can't wait to do it.

"Thanks, Jake. I'm really happy for you, too, man."

We hug and he smacks my arm as he heads to take his place in front of the guests.

Grandma's already where she's supposed to be. Jaxson sits beside her. We walk around them to take the seats beside him. Justin and Jason come around, and sit on my side. Jason tells me, "Drew's idea not to have bridesmaids and groomsmen. Her friend Bernie still isn't doing well."

"You mean the one—"

"—Yes, that one."

Justin leans forward and says, "Notice Jason doesn't have a date?"

"Fuck off, Justin," he mutters, low enough that Grandma couldn't hear him.

I ask, "Didn't work out?"

"Nah. Not the one."

"Thank God," Justin says. "I'd hate to have pretended to like her for the rest of my fuckin' life."

That wasn't said quietly.

"Language!" Grandma hisses.

Luna starts laughing under her breath, just before the music starts. I squeeze her hand and give her a kiss. "I love you."

"I'm sorry, but that was funny," she whispers.

Everyone stands up to watch Drew walk down the aisle. There's a lot of appreciative murmuring as an older woman walks with her. Jason whispers, "It's her mom, since her dad is the...you know."

"Ah." My eyes travel to Jake. He's gazing at his bride-to-be with pride and love.

Now that I think about it, I don't know if I've ever met a girl of his. It's a big deal for a woman to be brought home to the family, and Jake's the second youngest. He and I didn't hang out socially, so I didn't get to know who he dated.

"She's very pretty," Luna whispers. I nod, looking at the two of them coming together.

I remember the stories he told me about her when we were in Colorado. He did good with this one. She's a class act. What I really like is how she looks at my brother.

Drew kisses her mom's cheek and takes Jake's hand. They exchange a private look and a tear slips down her cheek.

I can't help it that my mind drifts after that as all the blah blah blah's are said.

It isn't until after the vows that my attention is grabbed, because when the pastor asks, "Who has the rings?" my dad stands up.

"I do."

Luna squeezes my hand as I go stiff. A knife turns in my chest because I know he wouldn't do this at my wedding. Not for me.

He hands Jake the rings and pats his arm, heading back for his chair. Jason glances to me and holds my look. I shrug like I'm not bothered. He stares a moment, seeing the truth.

The rings are slipped on and Drew's father says with a big smile, "By the power vested in me by the state of Georgia, I now you pronounce you husband and wife. You may kiss the bride."

Drew walks into Jake's arms and he kisses her like all of us Cocker brothers kiss our women, deeply and like no one is watching.

The crowd starts hollering their approval. Me and my brothers clap loudly, shouting things like, "Get 'er, Jake! Get 'er!"

Even Grandma whistles through two fingers. Luna is laughing and Jaxson leans over to tell her, "Welcome."

I glance over just as her head swings away from him. The look in her eyes is a puzzle to me, so I lean down. "What're you thinkin,' baby?"

Shaking her head like it's hard to say, she whispers, "How lucky you are."

"You're with me, baby. We're both lucky now."

LUNA

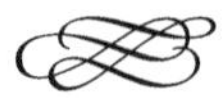

The dining tables are already set up, as pretty as if they were in a movie, with linens, bottles of both red and white wine on each, plus elaborate lavender and white floral centerpieces.

When the caterers begin removing folding chairs from the ceremony to make room for dancing after dinner, Jett and his brothers all pitch in to help. The five of them together makes me wish I could meet the sixth. They're all laughing and messing around, teasing about personal things.

None of them are quiet, except for maybe Jaxson. They shout things like, "Hey Jason, did it hurt you to not wear a hat, buddy?" and "Justin, you sure you want the Press seeing you do actual work here?" at which he shoots back with a grin, "I hope they capture this! Makes me look like a good guy!" Jaxson's deep voice dryly calls out, "Then we'd better stop."

They all lose it. And it goes on and on.

Jett looks so happy. It's obvious he's missed them like crazy. But from the way he keeps glancing to me, I know I'm part of the reason he's smiling like that.

I'm beginning to understand him more, and I think if I weren't here and hadn't stood up for him last night, he would be having a harder time being this near to his father.

Drew is making her way through the crowd. Some people she seems to know, others, not at all. She sees me and heads my direction, shaking hands as she comes, her beautiful white dress billowing behind her as a wind picks up the train.

With a happy smile, she introduces herself, "Hi, I'm Drew Ch...Cocker. Whoa, that feels really weird to say."

"Luna. Hi. I'm here with Jett."

"I know. I saw. Jake told me he's surprised."

"...Yeah..."

I'm not the best at normal chitchat.

"I just met him the other day for the first time, when he came home with Jake after the bachelor party so he could say hello."

Bachelor party?

On a quick glance to Jett as he stacks chairs, I instantly see him at a strip club.

He was a free man at the time.

Don't like how that image makes me feel.

Trying to push jealousy down, I blink back to her. "Oh, you guys live together?"

She laughs like it's hard for her to admit, "That's how we met. We were roommates."

My eyes widen. "Really? You didn't know each other when you moved in?"

"Nope," she grins, glancing to the brothers. "I was just as surprised as you are. It's a wild story. Those Cocker boys are somethin' else. Jake's...he's just wonderful." Turning back to me, she motions to what I'm wearing. "I love your dress."

"Nancy helped me pick it out." I glance down to finger the pretty fabric. I'm not a dress person, but I do feel good in this. More feminine. In this thing I'm very aware I'm a woman, which is normally never on my mind. I like it, but I prefer jeans over this any day.

"*Nancy* did?" Drew's happily surprised, and she asks me in a whisper, "Does that mean Jett and Michael worked things out?"

I guess she would think that, since it would imply a sort of friendship had happened. I'm not sure how Nancy feels about me now. She was polite today, but

I'm sure I offended her Southern sensibilities last night. Still, I'm not sorry.

I had to stand up for Jett.

He needed me to.

"Um...no. They didn't. But family can be a tricky thing."

Drew rolls her eyes in agreement, and glances over to wave at an older couple who are clearly waiting for her attention. Low enough that only I can hear, she confides, "Nancy and my mom are strugglin'. Little bit of a battle for who gets to do what, at the wedding. My mom lives a couple hours away. I think she's afraid of bein' replaced."

I'm sure all women who've lost their mother must be like me, just nodding and saying, "Mmmhmm. That's hard."

"It is. But they'll work it out. I have to go. My aunt Emma wants to talk to me. That's her over there."

I glance to the woman who was trying to get Drew's attention just a moment ago. She's got a scarf over her head, the kind those who are going through chemo have to wear. I don't ask about it, but I know from the sad look that just flickered over Drew's face that her aunt still isn't doing well.

"Are you stayin' in the city, Luna?"

"We're at Jaxson's place."

"Oh, I love him. He's so...*present*. Has a real calm

to him that I like. Jake looks up to him. Looks up to Jett, too. He talks about Jett like he's a god."

I can't help but feel intense pride at that.

"He *is* a god."

Drew thoughtfully stares at me, and nods. "I like you."

A surprised grin spreads my lips. "I like you, too, Drew."

"We'll talk again later?" she asks, reaching out to touch my forearm.

Reflexively I put my hand over hers. "Yeah."

She smiles and heads off. Her aunt greets her with open arms and I overhear a strong Southern drawl as she exclaims, "Drew, honey, you are just beautiful! Look at you! I'm so glad I was able to make it."

LUNA

Jett's waving at me to join him so I make my way through a crowd of strangers, most of them stealing quick glances to inspect the woman who stole Jett Cocker's heart.

A week ago I was riding alone on my bike from cheap motel to cheaper motel, sleeping on lonely beds, showering in badly lit bathrooms with miniature shampoos and soaps. I woke up every morning with a deeper gloom than I'd felt the day before. I ate by myself for every meal. Couldn't see the beauty around me. Didn't have anyone or anything except for that bike and the pain in my heart.

I shiver to think that I'd still be living like that if I hadn't taken this chance and faced the music of what I'd done. Said I was sorry. Took the leap of facing my fear of being loved, and being rejected if it was too late. I almost didn't try. Where would I be now?

Not somewhere as sunny as this with a man I love smiling at me like he is now.

No one has seen me like Jett Cocker has. Really seen me and accepted my flaws and loved me anyway. And while he had a head start at falling in love with me, I have fallen so hard that it hurts just to look into his eyes, I love him so much.

"Hey, Sunshine."

"Hi baby," I whisper, walking into waiting arms to receive a kiss.

"Now we eat. You hungry?"

"Uh huh. I'll try to be more dainty here."

He laughs. "Don't you fuckin' dare. You be you, baby. *You be you.*" His smile vanishes so quickly I look behind me to see what happened.

Michael Cocker is walking toward us. I see Nancy behind him, talking to guests, her mouth freezing mid-sentence from shock and worry as she notices her husband's path.

Jett's body has gone hard as steel.

Separating, we clasp hands.

His father's voice is somber and cautious. "Jerald..." He pauses, gathering his thoughts.

With his jaw tick ticking, Jett says, "Congressman."

Michael Cocker's eyes flicker. "I'm sorry I didn't invite you to the wedding."

I stare up at Jett and watch his Adam's apple move fast as he swallows hard. "I *was* invited."

"By your mother. But...it should have been by both of us."

Jett's taken aback, and handling it with little facial expression. "Okay."

"That's all I wanted to say. Have a good time." Mr. Cocker nods and glances to me, tipping his head as he turns to leave. He tucks his hands into his pockets, his back straight and his head slightly down as he contemplates what he just did. Nancy walks to him and in a voice no one can overhear, asks him what he just did. A relieved smile appears on her face and she glances over to Jett and nods. He answers her with the same.

Jaxson and the twins were still nearby so they got to see the exchange from that distance. Quick strides bring them to us, and all three ask, "What happened?"

Jett's fingers are still tightly around mine as he answers, "A truce."

They feel the weight of this news in different ways. Jason runs his hand through his hair like he can't believe it, and whispers, "That took a lot for him to do."

Jett is staring after his father. "It sure did."

Jaxson is staring at the grass. "I'll meet you guys at the table. I'm going to tell Jake what just went down."

"Thanks, man," Jett mutters. The twins both clap a hand on his shoulder and head off.

As soon as we're alone, Jett squeezes my hand in a way that tells me how much that meant to him.

He's a very masculine man.

I don't expect him to talk about it more.

I'm the same way, frankly, so I get it.

"Jett," I whisper.

He looks at me, grey eyes troubled.

"I'm going to eat like a fucking pig."

A grin explodes on his face and he laughs loudly, lifting up my chin, "Thank you, Sunshine."

"Any time."

The rest of the reception is a breeze.

JETT

It's only a nine-hour ride from Jaxson's place outside Atlanta, to South Vacherie, Louisiana, but there's no rush. God it felt good to have Sunshine's arms around me while I drove us to Birmingham Alabama. We just checked into Cobb Lane Bed & Breakfast, a converted old Victorian home that family friends told me about at the wedding.

The Ciphers usually stay at less romantic places, but I wanted somethin' with a little charm for this trip. It's the first time we've been together, alone, where I know she's not runnin' away.

"Ya like it?" I ask, as we walk into a bedroom with fringed antique lamps and a shiny, cream-colored blanket with a shit-load of pillows on it.

She grins. "I hope the walls are thick."

Chuckling, I toss the saddlebags on the hardwood floor. We had to ship her suitcase. Just brought enough for a one-night change of clothes.

"I've got somethin' thick for you, baby."

She sighs and meets me near the edge of the bed. "I know you do. Can't wait, because...it's just you and me now."

"And about twelve other people," I remind her, thinking how good it's gonna feel to bring her home where I'll watch her become part of the Cipher family for good.

"I mean, right now, Jett. It's just you and me."

I grab a fistful of her ass and draw her up on her toes to kiss me. We lash tongues and moan into each other until she surprises me by grabbing my hair and pulling my head back. "Did you go to a fucking strip club for Jake's bachelor party?"

"What if I did?"

Her dark eyes flash. "I will have to punish you."

"Can't wait for that."

She shoves me onto the bed and straddles me, untying her braid. "Jett, did you?"

"Mayyyyybe."

She slaps my chest then shakes out her hair with one hand, lifting up her shirt. "Did anyone have tits like these?"

Her bra is dipping with the weight of her luscious

double D's. I reach to grab 'em but she smacks me away, grabs my wrists and pins my hands above my head, grinding her crotch over my erection.

"You really think you can hold me down, woman?" I smirk. "I'm allowing this."

Her eyes are hooded as she grinds with me, our hips moving together. "You want to touch my tits, you have to tell me the truth."

"No one has what you've got." I smirk, then add, "ME," laughing at her reaction.

"You cocky fuck!"

"That's right!" I flip her over, mounting her so fast she yelps, eyes wide with shock. "See. I was allowin' you to pin me." Hovering my lips over hers, I use my thighs to spread her legs wide. "I didn't go to any fuckin' strip club, Sunshine. Anyone dancin' on that stage would have had your face on her and I was too pissed to go through that kind of torture."

She's gazing at me and moaning slightly as I grind into her. "Good," she breathes. That tone sends fire into my cock, and I can't wait anymore.

We get rid of our clothes while roughly kissing. She gives as good as she gets, that's what I love about fuckin' her. She's submissive sometimes, aggressive others. We just fit.

I fuck her on every surface of this place, just like I did that first night, the day we met.

We are covered in sweat, moaning incoherent, dirty things to each other.

When I finally have her in front of the antique bathroom mirror, thrusting deep as I can get in her dripping wet cunt for round number four, she locks eyes with me and stays there, cumming on my cock, body shaking.

Her eyes never leave mine.

She's totally open to me.

The fear is gone.

She's mine now.

And I am never gonna let the bitch go.

I cum so hard and so long that I am fuckin' whimperin' when it's done.

And I don't whimper.

"Look at you," she laughs. "Putty in my hands."

I'm catchin' my breath.

"Nah, just tired."

"Liar," she whispers with mischief in her dark brown eyes.

I grin at her through the reflection and while we're standing here with me inside her from behind, I pull her up and wrap my arms around her breasts, kissin' her shoulder. "I don't want you stayin' at the house."

"What?" she asks with a frown.

"I want you on the road with us. I want you to be a Cipher."

Her eyes light up and she grabs one of my forearms with both hands. "Really?"

"I already told Scratch. I need you *with* me, Sunshine."

She closes her eyes and starts biting her lips. A tear squeezes out and slips down her cheek, mingling with the dripping sweat like it was never there. "I need that, too."

Pulling out of her, I turn her around, reach over and grab a hand towel. She lays it on the counter, sits on it and wraps her curvy legs around my hips, locking her ankles above my naked ass and pulling me close while her hands rest on my sweaty chest.

"Jett...I'm scared of being this happy."

"Me, too," I rasp, kissing her. "But you're like me. If it ain't scary, it ain't fun."

"I love you, Jett Cocker."

"I love you so much, Luna, that I'm gonna give you a last name."

She stares at me and tilts her head up. I kiss her nose and get ready for round five.

JETT

TWO YEARS LATER.

My wife and I are in the backyard with Thai pads. I'm holding 'em at different degrees of angles so she can practice her kicks.

Her eye is a nasty shade of black and blue, and she's covered in sweat, wearing shorts and a tank top, her breasts held down with a sports bra and her hair back in a ponytail.

"Fuck!" she grunts as I hold 'em higher.

She kicks hard and then doubles over, grabbing onto her knees.

"I can't," she pants. "I have to stop a second."

"No! I'm not going to see your face all bruised up like that again."

"He surprised me," she says, side-eyeballing me while she catches her breath.

"Sunshine, listen up. I can't stand you gettin' hurt. You come out with us only if you stay safe."

"It's never really safe out there, with what we do. You know that."

Melodi calls out from the house, "Hungry yet?"

"Fuck no," Sunshine pants, shaking her head, eyes on the grass. "I don't feel good."

"Come on. Don't pussy out on me," I snap at her. To Melodi I call out, "Be there when we're through. Not a second earlier, so stop fuckin' askin'!"

Mel shouts, "Slave driver!" then goes inside, the old screen door clanking loudly behind her.

"Again!" I hit the Thai pads together. "Get up."

"I feel sick, Jett," Luna whispers.

"No no no. Come on. Get up."

"No...I really..." She steps away and turns her back on me, then vomits right there on the ground, mumbling, "Shit. Ugh."

I drop the pads and go to lay my hand on her back, my tone changing to worry. "What's goin' on? You okay?"

"No, I feel really sick, babe."

"MELODI!"

Within seconds, she's running down the steps, eyes on the puke. "Jesus, Jett! What'd you do to the poor woman?"

"I feel sick, Mel," Luna moans.

"No shit, darlin.' People don't lose their breakfast when they're at the top of their game." Guiding my girl upstairs, she throws me a scathing look. "This is your fault!"

I follow with my tail between my legs. Inside, Scythe and Honey Badger are watchin' NASCAR on T.V. They look over and see the women. "What happened?"

"Jett's an asshole, that's what happened," Melodi calls over. "Tyler, go get Luna some ginger-ale, honey.

"Okay, Mommy!" His spindly, growing legs take off for the kitchen.

"Where do you think you're goin'?" Melodi asks me as I follow them up the stairs. "Oh no. You stay down there. No woman needs her man to see her like this."

"She was a lot worse when she was in a fuckin' coma, Mel. I handled it pretty good then!"

"Just let me clean her up, Jett!"

"It's okay, Jett," Sunshine whispers, looking pale. "Just give me a second."

Clomping back downstairs I run into Scratch. "Luna's sick."

His salt and pepper eyebrows cock up. "She pregnant?"

I blink at him, then run back upstairs and bang on the bathroom door.

"JETT COCKER!" Melodi yells.

"LUNA! ARE YOU PREGNANT?!!"

There's silence on the other side. Melodi swings the door open and runs to her room.

Luna is sitting on the side of the bathtub, eyes big with fear of hoping it might be true. "Oh my God..." she whispers.

Melodi races back in, waving a pregnancy test.

I hear a door open behind me and Carmen and Tonk appear, half-dressed. "Did we just hear Luna might be pregnant?" Carmen asks, tucking in her shirt.

We just got back from a mission. Everyone is in the house and suddenly the second floor is full of Ciphers and their families.

We wait as Melodi stays by Luna while she takes that fuckin' test on the other side of the door.

Everyone is silent.

Honey Badger walks over and stands by me. I glance to him and he nods that he knows how much I want this.

One of Hannah's kids starts to say something and gets hushed.

I watch the doorknob turn.

Holy Fuck.

This is big.

What's she gonna say?

Melodi opens the door and her face is solemn. My heart sinks as Luna stands and walks to me, crying openly.

Never seen her cry in front of anyone but me before.

"Jett...I'm pregnant." Weeping, she falls into my arms and I start to cry, too, but mine is through laughter.

The whole place goes up in cheers.

Luna looks up at me, so overwhelmed she's almost devastated. "She was wrong. The gypsy was wrong."

"She sure fuckin' was, baby. She sure fuckin' was." We kiss and everyone just loses it. Shouting and whooping loudly. Banging on walls. Kids stamping their feet, even though little Celia doesn't know why she's doing it.

"Hey, Mel," I call over. "When you said it was my fault she puked...you were right. I take full blame." Melodi just makes a face, but she's grinnin' under it.

Luna burrows into my body, weeping quietly. I can

barely make it out when she whispers in my ear, "I get to be a mother!"

"You're gonna be the biggest badass mom who ever lived, Sunshine. And I can't wait to see it happen."

When Jake called to tell me he and Drew had a baby girl just a couple months ago, I knew it was comin.' The jealousy.

Hell, I knew from seven months before when he'd called and told me she was two months in.

That phone call about baby Emma really fucked me up for a couple days.

Never knew 'til I met my Sunshine I wanted to be a father, too.

I wanted it bad.

No protection and we fucked all the time, but it just wasn't gonna happen for us. We both began to believe it.

Luna and I rode our bikes out to Atlanta to see the baby. Dad and I were stiff with each other — he still hates my lifestyle — but everyone else was the same as always, happy to see me and thrilled Luna and I were still together.

They don't know we're never gonna be apart, that we eloped...got married in Vegas six months after Jake's wedding.

Someday I'll tell 'em.

No one was there except for Honey Badger and Jaxson, one to represent each family.

The Ciphers sure didn't like not being there, but I explained to their growling objections when we announced the news, that Luna and I aren't the big-wedding types. We didn't want the fluff. Hell, Elvis conducted our fuckin' ceremony just because it made us laugh.

After the wedding, when I said goodbye to Jaxson, he told me again he was happy to be there, but the brothers wouldn't understand. I nodded that I understood, and we hugged each other really hard.

When I called to say Luna and I were comin' to see the baby, I asked Jax to tell everyone not to ask Luna when she was gonna get pregnant.

People ask things before they think sometimes.

Not everyone can have babies, and that question can really stab you in the gut when you don't see it comin.'

He warned the family. People kept their mouths shut. But I saw Mom watching me starin' at my younger brother's new daughter. Her smile was sad, and it cut me in two.

After we got back, I had to let it go.

I told myself I had a love I never knew could happen to a loner like me.

I had a woman who rode a fuckin' motorcycle next to me, who kicked the shit out of sorry fucks who needed a wake-up call.

I had a teammate.

A best friend.

A lover.

All in one.

So I let it go, deciding, 'Shit man, don't be greedy. She's enough.'

But damn if this isn't a bonus.

While Luna showers off the sweat of her training, and the tears of her surprise, I walk out back to make a phone call.

My older brother picks up after two rings. "Hey Jett."

"Jax, guess what?"

"What?"

"I get to be a father!"

"No shit!?!!" he yells, happy as hell.

Staring at the waning sun slipping behind the tops of our oak trees, I tell him the story. Afterward we catch up on what's been going on in his life, with his woman.

He's always pretty tight-lipped, but he tells me some things that make me smile, and say, "I'm happy for you, Jax."

"If it's a boy, you're naming it after me, right?"

"Fuck no," I laugh as the screen door bangs behind me.

My wife smiles as she catches my happy gaze. "That Jaxson?" she asks, knowing he'd be the first one I'd call.

"Yep. Selfish prick wants the baby named after him."

Luna laughs and mutters, "Of course he does." Leaning into the phone, she tells him, "No way. Your head is big enough."

"I resent that," he shouts. "Congratulations!!"

Grinning, I say, "I'll call you later, Jax."

We hang up and I pull my wife into my arms and grin at her. Tears spring to her eyes as she stares up at me. "Dammit!" she whispers. "I can't stop crying. I just wept the whole time I was in the shower."

Emotion pulls at me as I nod and kiss her deeply.

"I hope it's a girl, Jett."

"Oh yeah? Why's that?"

"So I can name her after my mom." As Luna breaks down, I enclose her in the biggest hug I can, wanting to take all of her pain away forever for not having her mom, and all those years she thought she'd never conceive, all the times she watched the children here and wished one was hers.

Seven months later, her wish will finally come true. *Sofia Sol Cocker* is born, and rocks our whole world.

We gave her that middle name because Sol is the Spanish word for Sun, which is what our tiny, grey-eyed beauty is.

THE END.

After this sample of the Jaxson's second chance love story, Cocky Cowboy, there is a personal note from me.

COCKY COWBOY - RACHEL

As he empties the raw crystals into his paper cup, Ryan smiles his winning grin. "Rachel, the sooner we get back to Manhattan the better. This place, it's too fucking charming for me. I miss the grime."

I smile in an effort to release my mood. "We leave tomorrow evening. It's only one more night here."

"Can't we just go home today?"

From the look on his face he'd eat the cost and jump on a plane if I said yes.

I'm considering it. I'm having a shit time and want to go home, too. But only because of him.

Being back in the city I grew up in is very nostalgic for me and if I were here alone, I'd be having the best visit. Mom and I would be together at this market buying up everything and anything and laughing a lot.

I would have had those crepes, for example. I can still smell them. The strawberries and cream beckoned to me and I let them slip by.

After he comes in for another kiss, slipping his arm around my waist, the coffee held away from my Kate Spade dress, I sigh, "Maybe we *should* go home."

"Yeah?"

"But my parents wouldn't appreciate it."

He tempts me, "Who cares what they think," his voice low and husky.

Why the hell not? I feel like something's coming between he and I...or ending. I don't like seeing him how I do now. Part of me wants to rush to the airport and stick us back in New York where we were almost living happily ever after, especially by city standards. Most of our friends are single.

His iPhone beeps. As Ryan steps to the left to read the incoming email, the subject is put on hold.

I look away from him and in the distance, straight ahead, discover I'm being watched.

An incredibly sexy man is intently staring at me from within a neatly laid-out market stand filled with artisan cheeses.

He looks out of place in this city, like he'd be better suited on a ranch somewhere. He's dressed in a denim button-up shirt over equally faded blue jeans held up with a large, horseshoe belt buckle. It's visible only because a small section of his shirt is accidentally tucked in. The sun dances across his striking and ruggedly tan features, the kind of golden skin that only comes from working daily in the sun.

I cock my head trying to figure out where I know him from.

It's like he's daring me to remember.

He crosses his arms and keeps right on staring at me. As milliseconds pass his lips tighten, framed by several days worth of stubble. Emerald green eyes narrow as I hold his gaze.

My heart stops cold.

It can't be him.

No way.

He looks so different now I almost couldn't place him.

But yes.

It's him.

Oh my God.

Ryan swears at his phone as he types a reply with one thumb, but I don't see that because an invisible rope is slowly pulling me toward the man from my past.

An older white-haired lady is ignored as she asks him a question about his specialized product. She turns to see what's arrested his attention so completely and when she spots me in the same daze he's in, she moves to leave.

Neither of us noticed she was ever there.

After all these years...

Staring in wonder I breathe deeply in and whisper, "Jaxson Cocker."

Click here to download Cocky Cowboy and enjoy the strong and silent Jaxson Cocker's Second Chance Romance.

FROM ME.

When Jett showed up in Cocky Roomie, Book One, I knew he was badass. His motorcycle club saves people, and he is in opposition to his own father in order to do good in this world—in the way he believes it should be done.

I researched atrocities and came across Human Trafficking. I was shocked at how common it is in America. And that's how this story began.

I never plan plot. I sit down and start typing. So you'll find if you continue with the series that no story is formulaic. They don't follow traditional rules.

Not a fan of rules in general.

Somebody else made them up!

The Cocker family — overcoming real problems in

order to have happier lives, true love, better relationships of all kinds. Grab the 30 Day Free Trial and read them all free. All currently available in Kindle Unlimited.

Jett and Luna's Bonus scenes will melt you.

- You'll meet their daughter Sofia Sol as a child and see what happens to them as parents.
- Soph has her own book out now, and she's quiet the ride—Cocky Rebel.
- HONEY BADGER...my readers said he needed his own HEA. I listened, and gave them this novella, a Christmas story that can be enjoyed year 'round for a sweet and sizzling pick-me-up.

Rockstars, Athletes, MMA Fighters, Cowboys, Enemies to lovers Romance, Second Chances, Computer Genius, Billionaires, the list goes on with smart women and hot men fighting over who will fall first.

Because every real family is filled with variety. *#LiveWithLight. #FightWithLight.*

xx,

Faleena Hopkins

SPECIAL BONUS SCENES

Now available in Paperback: the collection of "future scenes" for the Cocker Brothers series, Books 1-16 together. These all take place after *"The End."*

LINKS TO:

YOUTUBE COVER MODEL INTERVIEWS

COCKY BOOKMARKS

SIGNED PAPERBACKS

COCKER FAMILY TREE

SPOTIFY — SERIES PLAYLISTS

HOT INSTAGRAM

http://authorfaleenahopkins.com

FACEBOOK GROUP

(SEARCH:) **COCKY READERS: COCKER BROTHERS**

Purely for true #cockerstalkers

Cocky Swag — Charity Project

https://teespring.com/stores/cocky-goodies

All 2017/2018 profits go to "K9s for Warriors," pairing pets with vets.

ALSO BY FALEENA HOPKINS

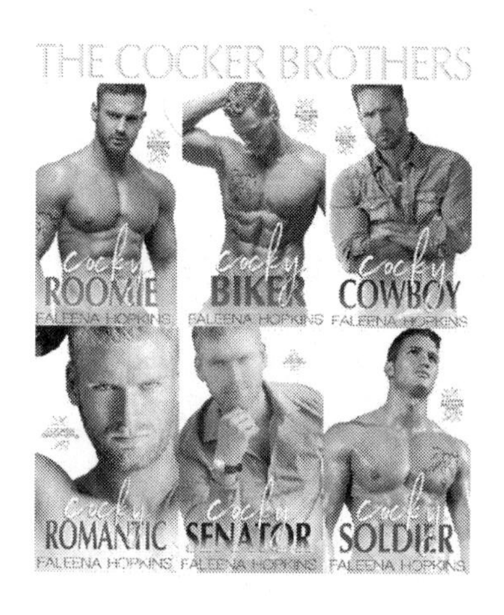

Series in Chronological Order:

(*Can be enjoyed out of sequence*)

Cocky Roomie - Jake Cocker

Cocky Biker - Jett Cocker

Cocky Cowboy - Jaxson Cocker

Cocky Romantic - Jason Cocker

Cocky Senator - Justin Cocker

Cocky Soldier - Jeremy Cocker

A Honey Badger X-Mas (Cocky Biker spinoff)

Cocky Senator's Daughter - Hannah Cocker

Cocky Genius - Ethan Cocker

Cocky Rockstar - Gabriel Cocker

Cocky Love - Emma Cocker

Cocky Quarterback - Eric Cocker

Cocky Rebel - Sofia Sol Cocker

Cocky By Association - Sean & Celia

Cocky Director - Max Cocker

Cocky and Out of My League - Nicholas Cocker

Cocky Bonus Scenes: Book 1-16

(more coming!)

Not in the Cocky Series

You Don't Know Me

A stand alone novel

Paranormal Romance

Werewolves of New York

Werewolves of Chicago

Owned by The Alphas

ABOUT THE AUTHOR

I've been writing since I was six-years-old when I sold my parents books for a dollar, written in crayon, hand illustrated to the best of my limited abilities, and bound with yarn by tiny, nail-bitten fingers.

Now today I'm also a filmmaker and actress. Stay tuned for the first feature film I'll be directing. The men have been doing that for decades (Woody Allen, Ben Affleck, Ed Burns, to name a few who act in their own projects), so why not give it a shot? I hope you'll be at my side for that. Should be a roller coaster of crazy.

Love, love, and more love,

xx,

Still curious about me? Here's my heart on my sleeve in a memoir blog post:
http://faleenahopkins.blogspot.com/2017/04/from-atlanta-to-new-york-city.html

A PLUME B

LUKE SKYWALKER CAN'T READ

© Kirsten McNally

RYAN BRITT has written for the *New York Times*, *Electric Literature*, *The Awl*, *VICE*, and *Clarkesworld* and is a consulting editor for *Story*. He was the staff writer for the Hugo Award–winning web magazine Tor.com, where he remains a contributor. He lives in New York City.

Praise for *Luke Skywalker Can't Read*

"Ryan Britt is one of nerd culture's most brilliant and most essential commentators . . . the Virgil you want to guide you through the inferno of geekery."

—Lev Grossman, author of the bestselling Magicians trilogy

"Ryan Britt is an uncontrolled experiment—a genre omnivore who has spent his time on this earth flying to other galaxies, undersea cities, freaky amusement parks, Middle Earth, Transylvania, Sherlock Holmes's London, and the Cretaceous. His essays are reliably smart, surprising, provocative, and funny."

—Karen Russell, Pulitzer Prize–nominated author of *Swamplandia!*

"Ryan mixes his love of sci-fi with his life story to produce one of the most witty, fun, warm, and insightful essay collections out there. If Luke Skywalker had a favorite book, it would be this one."

—Ophira Eisenberg, host of NPR's *Ask Me Another* and author of *Screw Everyone*

"*Luke Skywalker Can't Read* is personally revealing, effortlessly funny, carefully researched, and optimistic about the place of sci-fi/fantasy in the greater world of popular entertainment."

—Cecil Baldwin, narrator of *Welcome to Night Vale*

"Whether he's exploring paradoxes in *Back to the Future* and the fundamental illiteracy of the average Stormtrooper or being tied up and held over a rooftop by a couple of dominatrices, Ryan Britt is an amiable, perceptive, and highly entertaining observer of the sci-fi scene. I gulped down these essays like Dracula downing a pint of blood."

—Teddy Wayne, author of *The Love Song of Jonny Valentine*

"Sci-fi and fantasy fans, meet your new best friend. Ryan Britt has an encyclopedic knowledge of geek culture, from Aurebesh to Zardoz, and this collection of essays feels like you're hanging out with him at the world's nerdiest bar. *Luke Skywalker Can't Read* is smart, insightful, and totally fun."

—David M. Ewalt, author of *Of Dice and Men: The Story of Dungeons & Dragons and the People Who Play It*